WILD
VIOLENCE

D1458217

Blood Rites Horror presents
Wild Violence
a horror anthology supporting WWF UK

This edition published April 2021 by Blood Rites Horror.
All characters and events are fictional and any resemblance
to real people or places is coincidental.

Copyright belongs to the featured authors.

Please enjoy this book. Look out for future anthologies on
Amazon or go to bloodriteshorror.com for updates,
previews and more information. The editor and authors
featured are grateful for any reviews on Amazon or
Goodreads.

More from Blood Rites Horror

available now:

Bitter Chills   edited by Nick Harper
Parasite Gods   edited by Nick Harper
The Miracle Sin   by Marcus Hawke
This Lonely Carcass Song   by Nick Harper
Blood for a Cambium Heart   by Nick Harper
The SKITTERS series   by Nick Harper

coming soon:

April 30th	*Those You Killed* by Christopher Badcock
May 13th	*Thrall* by Nick Harper
July 1st	*Welcome to the Funhouse* edited by Kelly Brocklehurst and Jamie Stewart
September	*Pulp Harvest* edited by Nick Harper
December	*Camp Horror* edited by Nick Harper
January 2022	*Lore: Volume One* by Robert Cain

for details on anthology submissions and upcoming releases, please visit bloodriteshorror.com

WILD VIOLENCE

EDITED BY NICK HARPER

BLOOD
RITES
HORROR

CONTENTS

FOREWORD
by Nick Harper

There's a lot to be said for themes of nature and wildlife in horror. If you look to horror fiction from the late eighteenth century to early nineteenth, you'll find an abundance of stories that leaned into the "killer plant" trope as more and more exotic species were discovered; indeed, one of Sir Arthur Conan's only adventures outside of the Holmes catalogue was a short tale about a giant flytrap. If you look to the real world, and a little farther back, animal familiars were a distinct feature in certain witch trials; even now, because there is still a fear (as there always should be) in the unknown, and because new species are discovered all the time, there is horror in the wild.

But this is not the reason you're reading a nature-themed anthology right now. Oh, it makes for fantastic horror – and I'll get to the incredible stories we have in store for you in just a second – but the real reason we're here is that this is a book dedicated to supporting the WWF, a charity focusing on the conservation and protection of wildlife. This is a cause very dear to my heart and one that I'm truly proud to be supporting, and a huge thanks goes out to all our readers, and to everyone who has supported this book from its conception onwards. We all know the dangers facing our wildlife and our planet, and we're all aware of our own impact on that, and if we can do anything at all it is to learn and grow and provide what we can. If we can make even a tiny shred of difference with this book, thank you all.

And, of course, it wouldn't be possible at all without all the fantastic authors involved. It's incredible to see some people submitting stories time and again and helping us to support some wonderful causes (if you haven't checked out our *Parasite Gods* anthology yet, take a look – every penny of profit goes to Cancer Research), and I'm thrilled to say that *Blood Rites* regulars Spencer Hamilton and Carla Eliot are back again, as well as *Bitter Chills* closer Patrick Whitehurst; Hamilton with an insightful, descriptive and genuinely horrifying tale that I believe really sets the tone for the rest of the book; Eliot with a new take on a *very* old story that'll leave you wondering long after, and that gives us horror in the form of a particular garden and a particular example of humanity; and Whitehurst with a claustrophobic desert scramble reminiscent of those early exotic-plant stories.

And, as always, it's an absolute pleasure to welcome some new writers to the family: Aiden Merchant presents a wonderfully vivid post-apocalypse with *Islands of Trees,* and poet Grace Reynolds takes advantage of the real-life horrors in nature in *Inside Out.* In fact, that's just another part of what makes nature-themed horror so thrilling – the idea that, even with no supernatural force or crazed mind involved, there's always something out there that can hurt you.

Speaking of hurt, look out for Sarah Roberts' and Michael Benavidez' *Descent,* in which an especially persistent rat plagues our haunted main character and twisted, visceral language is used really quite beautifully; Michael R. Goodwin's *Power Lines* brings us more wonderful imagery and horrific beasts, and *The Perigean Turn* brings nature right out of the water for a spooky coming-of-age tale. We're back to the forest for Mocha Pennington's *Over the River* and across the globe for a brilliant take on ancient lore with *Krodha* by J.D. Keown; and with L. Pine's *Furry Skins,* a hunter is confronted by strange creatures. This is what *Wild*

Violence is all about; not only the weirdness and the horror found in the everyday, in nature, right outside – but also what we can learn from that outside world, and from the horrors we might have inflicted upon it.

So thank you, once again, for supporting this book and for helping us to make a difference. Enjoy the stories within and be sure to follow and support all our authors (you can find out more at the back of the book) – but most importantly, be careful out there.

You never know what's lurking in the weeds.

Nick Harper
Norfolk, England

THE OVERNIGHT FOREST
by Spencer Hamilton

It grew overnight, the forest in Vatican City.

Many whispered that they heard it in the night, pushing up through the paving stones of the Piazza San Pietro, groaning like some long-slumbering village of giants stretching into wakefulness, branches shushing against the stone of the Tuscan colonnades. But Paolo did not believe them. He would turn seventy years old come the spring, and hadn't had a restful sleep in years. His hearing, on the other hand, was perfectly fine, and he hadn't heard a thing. Not over the usual susurrus of passing guards and the distant ocean's roar of that Eternal City, the surrounding Rome.

No, it had arrived in silence, perhaps even at the blink of an eye. Paolo believed the forest to be the will of God the Almighty Himself, and if He wished for the sun to set on the square but rise on the forest, then it

11

would be so.

Paolo stared into the gloom of the forest. He stood at the bottom of the steps leading to the basilica, the ceremonial cape of watered silk discarded at his feet, marveling at how much had changed overnight. Not just in the piazza, but in the Church itself. They had moved fast, in the early grey hours of the morning; the Swiss Guard had erected tall, finely meshed barricade walls across the great expanse of road connecting Vatican Hill to the heart of Rome. Beyond that, a caravan of hulking firetrucks and *polizia* barring entry from reporters and news vans and turned devout believers away from their pilgrimage.

The Vatican had shut itself from the world.

It was not just the forest the Church wished to hide.

Paolo glanced up and around at the loggia of the blessings, the balcony from which the new Holy See of Rome would be announced.

Today is a day of sorrow... and punishment.

The Pope was dead. Along with the forest, his corpse had been found just hours ago. A crimson flower had bloomed across his left breast – a burst heart. Paolo had not lain eyes on him, but it was said that his hawkish, Argentinian features were stretched in a death mask of indescribable horror, as if he had been given a peek of the brimstone of Hell and all its festering demons and his heart burst from the fright.

On closer inspection, the medical examiner claimed to have found a nest of thorns tangled around the chambers of his heart like barbed wire.

Paolo believed they were witnessing the wrath of God, finally descending upon the Church after its long corruption of power. The Lord's innocent children, touched and groomed and raped and tortured by the very men who claimed to be His appointed. Paolo would never admit this, but in his heart he was glad of that crown of thorns in the late Pope's chest; every day that man failed to swiftly condemn and account for the Church's sins against those children was another barb in Jesus's crown. Another nail in His flesh. To rape a child was to rape Mother Mary herself. And the Catholic Church had become a sanctuary for rapists.

The Holy See had his chance, Paolo thought bitterly. *Now the Lord our God has taken it into His own hands.*

Paolo's vestments rasped a soft rhythm against the stone as he stepped closer to the shelter of the trees. Other cardinals called him crazy for coming near the forest, said a score of guards had marched inside and never returned – said he would anger God. But God was already angry. To cower now would be to deny responsibility.

The travertine of the paving stones shone white beneath the gloom of the canopy. The limestone had split and buckled and given way to the questing roots of the trees. Black soil peeked through, soil that looked slick with decay, and already a bed of leaves lay in mulchy drifts. It was dark beneath the tangle of branches, impossibly so, as if in defiance of the sun climbing in the blue sky. A weighty silence reigned, cotton balls pressing themselves into his eardrums, cutting his tether to the outside world. It felt to Paolo as though he were entering a new realm. Even the air tasted different here: cloying; heavy. It left a film of decay on his tongue that he dare not scrape off. He would accept whatever discomforts his God deemed fit.

It embarrassed Paolo that he was not a learned man when it came to God's natural creation. He did not know the names of trees indigenous to the Italian coast, but surely these were not those trees. Surely, for that matter, had these trees never seen Earth's light. They were grotesque. Wide, rubbery trunks that soared up like twisted columns, their skin a nasty dark brown, almost black, that seemed to give off a red light beneath glimpses of sun. It looked as if the bark were merely translucent, a skin to house the pulsating blood beneath. Veins appeared to throb beneath the bark, so that the entire forest looked to pulse together; *thump-thump*, *thump-thump*, a giant, sluggish heart. Worse than this was the thick black sap, like rancid molasses, seeping from wounds in the trunks. Paolo was afraid to go too close, but just as his hearing was perfectly fine, so was his eyesight, and he could make out large, unrecognizable insects encased in the dripping gobbets of sap.

Strange things had been happening in the Vatican all morning. Large swathes of the botanical gardens had shriveled up and died. Entire hectares of land were disfigured and malformed with blight. Just walking within the perimeter of the Giardini Vaticani was enough to send cankerous lesions erupting across your skin.

The gardeners whispered of Chernobyl, of radiation poisoning, of death and disease.

Paolo felt eyes on him, boring down from along the top of the colonnades: the one hundred forty saints circling the piazza. On this morning their statues seemed so much more attentive, somehow lively. As if they were considering bounding down onto the paving and joining him in the forest.

Indeed, he had noted when first coming upon the forest that one of the two pedestals flanking the basilica steps now stood conspicuously empty. St. Paul was right where he belonged, naturally, but St. Peter... in his place, where he had stood guard for hundreds of years, now sat only crumbled stone; potholes led away and into the trees in impossibly long strides.

It sent a shiver down Paolo's spine.

The forest grew thicker as he walked, until he had to pick up his robes so he could lift his feet clear of the tangling underbrush with every step. Branches knitted together high overhead. It was near night, just a dozen strides past the outer ring of trees. Light refused to penetrate. Shadows lay thick like spiderwebs, shadows that twisted and twined around him in a capering dance, though the air was suffocatingly still. He wanted more than he'd wished for anything in his long life to turn and run, screaming, from this place.

But I am here, Lord. I open my heart to You. I ask for Your forgiveness.

Paolo was on a mission – not a mission from God but rather *for* God.

In the mayhem of the morning, Paolo had only made it a few steps into the Casa Santa Marta before a swarm of people had surrounded him, all buzzing like a hornet's nest. He had come to see that the Pope was properly informed of the forest which had somehow sprung from nothing all through Piazza San Pietro and to advise him on the matter – what to do about the press, what to do if the trees suddenly encroached upon the basilica – but it seemed not only that someone had beaten him to the pope's suite but that there was now more urgent news.

The Holy See of Rome, sovereign of the Vatican City State, *dead*?

'His heart,' a boy stammered, his face, peeking out from the small crowd surrounding Paolo, sweaty and white as a sheet, 'it – it – just... *burst*! Like a bladder! *Dio –*'

A stern vulture of a man hushed the boy, dismissed him, turning his attention to Paolo with grave importance. This was Cardinal Giuseppe Brizio, the Secretary of State and head of the Roman Curia – and constantly flaunting this title of office in Paolo's face. Paolo did not like the way the man treated that young boy, and he wondered then, just as he had wondered a thousand times, what degree of stain was surely on Brizio's soul.

What part do you play in the Church's sins, Cardinal? he

thought. *Have you found yourself alone in a room with a child and thought even God could not see? Have you looked the most monstrous of our priests in the eyes and assured them they would be transferred and their abominable acts against God's children would be swept under the rug that is the power and might of the Vatican?*

But Paolo had never spoken his thoughts aloud. And now the Almighty had come to collect.

'We must act quickly, Paolo,' Brizio said. 'We cannot let the Church fall in its darkest hour.'

Paolo snorted now, as he walked deeper into the forest and thought back on Brizio's pompous proclamations. The Church's darkest hour. Darker than the centuries-long hour that was the Holy Inquisition?

This Church's hands boiled themselves in blood a long time ago, Paolo thought grimly. *Blood cannot be covered up. It brings flies and maggots and infection. It must be scrubbed clean, and to do so we must accept that it is blood.*

He had told that sanctimonious Brizio as much that morning, if in more diplomatic words.

'If we are to move forward into the light of the Lord,' he had said, glaring fervently at his fellow cardinal, 'then we must not look at a sign from God and call it a scandal that must be covered up. Too much covering up has been done by that man.'

The half-dozen or so faces surrounding him in the Domus Sanctae Marthae curdled in horror, as if Paolo had uttered blasphemy. But it was no such thing. The Pope was not God; the Pope was a man – a man who, like others before him, was now facing judgment from on high. No future pope would follow in their footsteps if Paolo had anything to say about it.

'Do not clutch at your pearls as if it is not something we all know in our hearts,' he'd said, his voice trembling just below a rumble. 'We will say thanks to our Heavenly Father for blessing us with this warning, and we will act swiftly in penance, or we accept that the Roman Catholic Church will not live to see the second coming of Christ.'

His words echoed in the silence that had followed. They all knew what would happen when the College of Cardinals arrived to begin the papal conclave: they would elect Paolo as the next Pope. It would be unanimous and it would be among the shortest conclaves in history. This had been an accepted fact for several years now.

'What would you have us do?' Brizio said, finally breaking the spell. His face, surprisingly, did not show resentment toward Paolo for his assumed authority. It gave Paolo a certain amount of begrudging respect for the pompous ass.

'Nothing,' he responded, looking at each person in turn. 'Help to ease the panic if you must. I, on the other hand, have an urgent meeting of paramount importance in the Piazza San Pietro.'

Oh, they had all tried to stop him.

Cowards, every one, he thought in disgust.

When at last he came to a spot where he had to carefully choose his path lest he become trapped between the now entangled, grotesque trees, there came a noise.

He stopped.

Frantic panting. The acoustics of the forest were deceitful, thrown in every direction so that it seemed almost as if the person making the panting sounds were whizzing in impossibly fast arcs around Paolo. As he paused to listen, he noticed an undercurrent of deep, ancient groaning, and he imagined then that these unnatural trees were somehow *aware*, were like bullying children, and were stretching their blood-black branches to pluck the panting man from the ground and swing him through the turgid air.

The panting wheeled its way closer and was joined by a scuffling through the understory of the forest –

outcries of pain, thudding sounds that could only be this person slamming into the trunks of the trees as he ran. Paolo grimaced at the thought. Those sickening trees... he expected they would feel unbearably warm to the touch, just waiting to slough off their skin and bury you in iron-tasting carrion sap, your drowned corpse joining those of the impossibly large insects...

Paolo shook his head violently. 'Get a hold of yourself,' he uttered.

He waited for the man to burst into sight, but eventually the sounds receded; the air was heavy and still once more. His cassock was soaked through with sweat. He was suddenly grateful he had chosen to shed the heavy scarlet *ferraiolo* at the entrance to the basilica.

Somehow, this new silence was more frightening than the panting and scuffling. It spoke of intent. Some deep anger welling up from the earth and boiling the air. Sweat stung his eyes. His hands began to shake, which was new for Paolo, even at his advanced age. In a past life, before he took up the cloth, he was a surgeon and prided himself in his steady hands.

But now, they shook. In fear, they shook.

'Our Father, Who art in Heaven,' he whispered into the stillness, grasping his hands together, 'hallowed be

Thy name; Thy kingdom come; Thy will be done –'

His voice clogged in his throat, and he fought the desperate urge to cough, to spew the sickly air from his lungs. A wild thought occurred to him then, that this forest, this overnight forest in the Piazza San Pietro, home of that martyr Saint Peter, *was* His kingdom come upon the earth; indeed, that the Pope's violent death was His will. Yes, these were all conclusions Paolo had come to already, but the sheer weight of them, the gravity of his God's anger, suddenly pressed down on his shoulders and he fell to his knees, sinking into the mulch and sending a wash of decay to his nostrils.

'Father... please...' He raised his voice. *'Hallowed be Thy name!'*

A man burst from the trees and Paolo screamed.

The first he saw was the colors of the Medici swimming out of the darkness: the vibrant blue, yellow, and red of the Swiss Guards' uniforms. The young man ran straight toward Paolo, tripped on an exposed root – *was that root raised a moment ago?* Paolo's mind gibbered – and slammed into the ground. His hat tumbled from his sweat-slicked blond hair. He looked up, a mere foot from where Paolo knelt, and stared wildly. A bloody handprint had imprinted itself across his left cheek, the index finger welling one eye with a single red tear.

'*Tua eminenza,*' the young man whispered, his voice a dry croak. '*Per favore, vostra eminenza...*'

From between his shoulder blades rose a halberd, quivering as its blade stuck firm through his spine and organs and meat. He seemed to be unaware of its presence.

'Son,' Paolo said in Italian. 'Where are your brothers?'

'My brothers,' he repeated, eyes wild yet unseeing. 'My brothers... they are alive.' He swallowed. 'How are they alive?'

'Up, son,' Paolo replied, not bothering to answer the boy's question. He was clearly in shock, and who could blame him with a halberd treating his insides like a sheath? '*Up* we go.'

Paolo grasped the boy by the shoulders and together they clambered awkwardly up. He brushed slimy leaves from his clothing, though the guard did not bother doing the same. Instead, he stared blankly down at the blade tip protruding from the center of his chest. It was a silver spike a good ten inches long, pushing clear through his body and glistening with his viscera. Paolo deduced that this would put the crescent axe and the filigreed hook somewhere deep in his chest. How was there room for all that metal alongside the lad's heart and lungs and arteries? How was he standing at all?

'The others, son,' Paolo said, snapping his now steady hands in front of the guard's face. 'Take me to them.'

Still with that uncomprehending look on his face, the young Swiss Guard with the handprint of blood on his cheek and the halberd through his chest turned and led Paolo through the forest. Though he had run helter-skelter through the trees, he seemed to have no trouble picking his way back from where he came and to his brothers.

The noises reached them first – more scuffling and panting, but above that, screams, and beneath, a slow dirge of zombified groaning. At random intervals, all this was overcome by the loud slam of something impossibly heavy shuddering the very forest floor.

They came upon a clearing, and Paolo was momentarily grateful to see something he recognized: the Maderno fountain, which meant they were on the north side of the piazza.

Then he saw the blood.

It gushed from the large fountain in the place of

water, winking darkly in the sunlight as it rose into the air like a veritable river. Gouts of it splashed five, six meters high, then cascaded down onto the inverted *vasque*, a mushroom cap of stone and sparkling tile.

Playing in the blood-filled basin like children were the young guard's brothers, all in their matching uniforms. Only they weren't playing. They were using the fountain as a staging ground for their defense against the enemy.

The enemy... Dear God!

Even taller than the fountain was the stone giant attacking – *massacring* – the Swiss Guard. The giant wore flowing robes that bent stiffly as he moved, as if unsure whether to be stone or fabric. His weary features were framed by tight curls and a full beard. In one hand he held what looked to be two large keys, glinting silver and gold in the sun; the other held a halberd, which looked comically small in his grasp as he plunged it into a screaming guard and submerged him in the fountain's pool of blood.

But the guard never stopped screaming. Even under the red, frothing surface, even when he surely must have run out of air and had to fill his lungs with the blood. Even, as he scrambled from the fountain's reservoir and from the living statue, when the halberd ripped his bowels from him and they streamed out like garland, still he screamed.

They won't die, Paolo realised. *Oh, why won't they die?!*

The guard still moved to escape, climbing over the fountain's octagonal stone lip. As he did so, his intestines spooled out further, twitching like live wire.

Paolo wrenched his eyes from the fountain and stared all around at the bodies littering the ground. Bodies that still moaned and crawled about as if in a daze, despite missing limbs and insides and litres of blood. Here the paving was mostly intact, away from the questing roots of the trees, and it was painted in bright splashes with the Swiss Guards' hot blood.

There came a squelching sound, and Paolo found himself staring open-mouthed at a guard just a few strides away. The young man – he couldn't be more than twenty years old – sat with his upper half on the paving stones in a puddle of his own blood. His lower half had been ripped off at the waist and was nowhere to be seen. Yet still the man moaned, alive, as he stared down at his stomach in disbelief and tried stuffing his intestines back inside his torso.

Squelch. Squelch.

It was a quivering mess in his hands, shiny and wet, and it fell again and again from the hole at the bottom of his body – and again and again he picked it all up and stuffed it back in, making that horrible squelching noise. Like dragging a heavy rope through mud.

'*Aiuto!*' a voice muttered. It was a scream that didn't have enough air. '*Aiutami! Por favore...*'

Paolo's eyes dropped from the halved guard to his own feet and he jumped back in horror. His right calfskin penny loafer had been pressing into the soft flesh of a young man's cheek. He'd felt the man's pleas for help against his toes as an insistent vibration.

This guard... he had no body.

His neck was a ragged mess, the delicate white of his spinal cord blending almost perfectly with the travertine of the paving stones. His eyes swivelled in their sockets, wide with fright, and then locked with Paolo's.

'*Aiutami,*' he said, his voice strangely bled of any substance. '*Por favore...*'

That final plea, from a decapitated head, was what broke Paolo's resolve. He turned from the undying carnage and he ran. This time, as the dark of the forest enveloped him again, he thought of it as a blessing, as a shield against unfathomable evils. The dim heaviness of the air was almost welcoming. It was as if those mysterious trees were stretching out their black, rubbery boughs and embracing him.

The Piazza San Pietro was designed nearly four centuries before by the Italian architect Bernini, and its elliptical shape and surrounding rows of Tuscan columns were said to evoke the "eternal arms of Mother Church" as she embraced the Vatican's many guests.

But these trees... this infernal forest... this was no welcoming embrace. Eternal, perhaps. Eternal damnation. If the colonnades were the arms of Mother Church, then these trees were the raking claws of Mother Nature. This was an old evil – older than the earth from which its roots sprung, older even than time itself, maybe. Perhaps time did not exist under such a canopy.

Paolo wanted to look over his shoulder but could not.

Those boys, he thought. *Those poor young lads...*

How long had he been here? How long since he first stepped into this shadow realm? Had more tragedies erupted throughout the greater Vatican? Already he was having trouble remembering what the proper place looked like, with its gorgeous, sweeping art teleporting its residents to a more godly time. The basilica – the last place he'd visited before coming here. Stepping through its soaring halls and out to the steps leading down to the forest.

He'd stood there, a light breeze playing with the whisp of white hair still clinging to his head – he'd kept his hearing and his eyesight and his steady hands, but not his hairline – preparing himself for what he must do. Preparing for that final journey down the grand steps and into the forest to speak to God and do as He would have him do. But first, a tap on his shoulder.

'Your eminence?'

He turned to find, of all the people who could have come to talk him out of this crazy mission, the sweaty boy from the Domus Sanctae Marthae who had first uttered the circumstances of the Pope's death. He was sweatier now than ever, positively drenched in his servant's uniform. He held in his hands –

Paolo snorted. 'What's your name, boy?'

'Lorenzo.'

'Lorenzo.' Paolo nodded. 'Strong name. And what's this, then?'

The boy gulped. 'I... thought you'd want to, you know, since you're –'

'Spit it out, boy.'

'I thought you'd want your full attire to go and meet God.' The boy's voice cracked on the last word.

Paolo nodded again. 'Very well. Let's have it.'

With only a moment's hesitation, the boy jumped into action: first, he lifted onto his tiptoes and placed the *zucchetto* and then *biretta* upon Paolo's head, trapping the whisp of hair beneath. That done, he gathered a heavy cape from where it hung over his shoulder and made to tie it around the cardinal's neck. Paolo smiled and obliged, holding his chin out as the boy tied a bow beneath it.

As he tied, the boy started, 'Your eminence – '

'Call me Paolo, son.' At the look of terror on Lorenzo's face, he added, 'I insist. On a day such as this, let you and I be on equal footing.'

He'd hoped for this to elicit a grin, but the boy seemed vexed. 'P-Paolo...'

'Yes, Lorenzo?'

The boy wiped a bead of sweat from the tip of his nose. 'Are you not afraid?'

Yes, he thought. The truth was that he was utterly terrified.

But what he said was, 'There is nothing to fear at the hands of the Lord.'

'Yes, well...' The boy cleared his throat, which had cracked again. 'That is what I was thinking, too. So don't you think... the Pope, the Gardens, *that*,' – he nodded down the steps toward the forest – 'haven't you wondered if those are maybe not at the hands of the Lord? That perhaps it's something... evil?' He glanced around, like just saying the word on Vatican grounds would be means for a smiting.

Paolo raised a steady hand and placed it on the boy's shoulder. In doing so, the cape rose where it rested against the cardinal's arm. He nodded down at it.

'You see this *ferraiolo*?'

The boy eyed the cape in confusion, but nodded.

'Do you know why it is red?'

'Because of your title, Cardinal.'

'Don't be so simple,' Paolo snorted. 'It and all of my vestments are red – are *cardinal* – because of the blood I am willing to shed for my faith. And so, whatever happens in those trees? I am willing.'

Lorenzo nodded, though before a smile could find its way across his face he grew pale once more – paler, perhaps, than ever before. He was eyeing something over Paolo's shoulder.

'Your em– er, Paolo... San Pietro is gone.'

Paolo squeezed the boy's shoulder so that his hand wouldn't shake.

'Yes. Perhaps he will protect me in the forest. Now

go.'

Perhaps it's something... evil.

Lorenzo's words came back to Paolo now as he fled the nightmare at the fountain. How could what he just witnessed be anything other than the work of evil? To do such unspeakable violence against those innocent young members of the Swiss Guard...

But no. Wasn't that exactly what the Church itself was doing? Unspeakable acts against innocent children? Paolo would do well to remember the Old Testament. An eye for an eye. God slaughtered all His creation – men, women, and children. His wrath fell on those who did not act swiftly. If He could send a flood to baptize the earth, He could send a forest to the Vatican.

It was nearly black in this part of the forest. No light penetrated the leaves above, and Paolo found himself stumbling from trunk to trunk in his desire to get away. A part of his mind made the connection, in a vague, detached sort of way, that he was now mirroring the actions of the young Swiss Guard who had first found him and brought him to the fountain: stumbling blindly through the dark in horror from the things he'd seen in the light, crying out with each thud against the throbbing, pulsing boles and boughs of the trees.

The air lightened in almost indiscernible degrees, until Paolo saw that he was nearing another clearing. A scream rose in his throat at the thought of what carnage he might stumble upon this time, but he choked it down. He was newly awakened now, shaking his doubts away like foggy sleep. He would see this through; he would find his God and he would beg for forgiveness and he would do what needed to be done to dredge the Church out of this Hell of its own design.

What he found was a clearing far larger than the one surrounding the fountain, and at first glance it looked as if he had stumbled upon the ancient ruins of some Cyclopean city. Massive chunks of cut stone lay scattered like a toppled Stonehenge. In the centre of it all rose a behemoth chunk of grey stone that ended far above his head in a mess of crumbles and cracks. It tickled something familiar in his brain.

He wove between the ruins. Each block rose above his head, as tall as a house, solid red granite smoothly hewn and clean of any glyphs or carvings. Block after block, smashed to the earth in mini craters of cracked and upheaved paving stones. Some had toppled atop others and fallen akimbo, leaning in a crumbling wreck.

He knew before he reached the center of the clearing that he had found the obelisk. The *Vaticano*. Soaring twenty-five meters straight up toward the heavens to proclaim for all to see: *Behold the Cross of the Lord!* Here it lay in ruins, after so many centuries. Paolo could have wept if he wasn't still in shock from the events at the fountain. This had been the only obelisk in all of Rome that still stood since ancient times. Caligula had brought it here for Nero's Circus, and now, centuries later, it was the Holy See that had brought it crashing down.

In Paolo's many years living in the Eternal City, he had lost count of the times he'd come to the Piazza San Pietro just to visit the obelisk. He loved how it functioned as the gnomon of a giant sundial, casting a clockwork shadow around the square as if San Pietro himself kept perfect time for the pilgrims of the Church. He loved those bronze lions –

He froze. The lions! He strained his head, wincing against the bright, piercing sunlight after so long in the dark, to gaze at the top of the *Vaticano* base.

Nothing.

He whipped his head around, half-expecting to see giant golden lions pouncing upon him, their manes green with *verdigris*. But he was alone.

Still, his body remained on high alert as he circled the still-standing base of the obelisk. As he came to the east-facing side, a word carved into the stone jumped out at him. The rest had been obscured by crawling vines of wet, sickly purple that had thrust up and around the stone as if consuming it. But the single word was clear enough:

FVGITE...

Flee!

But he did not. He could not.

As he came to the south side of the clearing, he found that he could not go on. On this side of the toppled obelisk, the ground was impassable. The paving had been demolished, pushed out from beneath so that it resembled the gnashing teeth of a giant buried in the earth. Indeed, it *looked* as if a giant had recently climbed from its grave: huge furrows of earth had been scooped from Vatican Hill, fissures that ran jaggedly across the clearing and hissed shimmering gases. That sense of an ancient evil overcame Paolo again, and for a moment he looked back at the broken Egyptian obelisk and thought of gods long dead but risen again – Set... Mafdet...

Sekhmet...

Do not entertain such thoughts! Paolo chastised himself. This was no Ancient Egyptian evil. This was the result of an entire forest of monstrous trees bursting from the earth in a single night. This was God's will.

But as he picked a new path around the massive pits in the piazza, he found that he still was not convinced. He was not convinced that these particular holes were the product of the trees questing up from below. For one, there weren't many trees nearby, this close to the obelisk's base. But for another, they did not appear to be newly dug. It seemed to Paolo that he was peering down into something that had existed long before last night, perhaps even centuries... or longer. A smell wafted up from them, one he struggled to pinpoint. Dusty, yes, and with a hint of... incense? Yes, more than a hint. Yet beneath that refreshing scent lay an undercurrent of malaise.

A voice in his head whispered, *The smell of a graveyard!*

He reached the far side of the clearing, now a stone's throw from the obelisk base with all those excavated tunnels in between, when he saw it. Lying partially inside the farthest hole was a cross, its beams larger than Paolo's body. A patina of pale green had eaten away at its bronze surface. The cross that once crowned the obelisk, somehow fallen clear on the opposite side from the rest of the monument. It had come to rest, in this grave-like hole, upside-down.

Paolo froze, staring down at it. It was believed that Saint Peter himself was crucified upside-down. On the other hand, some believed the inverted cross was a sign of disrespect from the Devil. He thought of that gigantic statue ripping the Swiss Guard limb from limb and realised he didn't know which belief he would prefer.

A hand crawled out like a spider onto the bottom of the cross.

Paolo's entire body gave a jolt. Not a sound escaped him.

He watched, still frozen, as this hand, impossibly small against the large cross, was joined by another. Hands of pale flesh smudged with dirt, their fingernails blackened with the stuff and strangely long and jagged. The hands jerked and twitched in bursts of disjointed movement. It was unnatural. Wrong.

His mind gibbered nonsensically, *It's Peter! Climbing down from his own crucifixion!*

The hands gave one final heave and the rest of their

body came into view.

It was a child.

Paolo screamed.

A boy, no older than seven or eight, clambering out of the pit in the earth with the help of the fallen cross. His mud-caked hair fell to his shoulders. The rest of his body was sunken like a mummy's. It spoke of death and decay, and had lain in the dirt for so long as to have forgotten even the memory of life. The boy's clothes were now no more than rags, and his immodesty embarrassed Paolo. He wanted to wrap him in a blanket and take him to hospital.

But those eyes... *those eyes!*

Sunk deep in their sockets, still they gleamed, like eldritch bog fire. Dancing pinpricks of red the colour of his cape, abandoned at the steps to the basilica. They seemed to laugh at him, at his horrified rictus expression, at the way his hands raised involuntarily as if to cover his eyes but froze in the forest's cloying air. The nose beneath those eyes was just a pit of sunken flesh and bone, and beneath that, the boy's mouth stretched into a knowing grin. Black, glistening sludge seeped over cracked lips and a dehydrated slug quested out to slurp it up.

A gurgling laugh issued from the boy's torn,

parchment-paper throat.

'Come to gloat, Father?' the boy asked.

Paolo gave no reply. He could not.

'Come to see what power you wield?' the boy asked. He continued his spiderlike, jerking crawl up the side of the inverted cross. 'Come to see all the little boys and girls you and yours have manipulated like puppets? Just grease that hole, stick your fist in, and move our mouths to say what-*eeeeeev*-er you want!'

Another set of hands burst out of the hole less than a meter from Paolo's feet. The bony fingers gripped the shattered paving stones at the edge and hauled a second child out of the dark, just as dead – yet just as impossibly alive – as the first.

Another scream ripped itself from Paolo's throat and he fell, landing hard on his rear. He was only dimly aware of the stiff, boxy *biretta* as it tumbled from his head and disappeared in the underbrush. He kicked his loafers against the torn-up paving until he was out of reach of the second child.

He stared, numb, as children dredged their corpses up and out of the ground. Children everywhere, some missing limbs, some crawling on naked bone. One little boy or girl – he could not tell – had their head so crooked on their neck that it leered at him nearly upside down, like the inverted cross. The children's skin was parchment-thin and clung tightly to their withered abdomens so that their spinal columns poked through from the other side.

Paolo finally found his voice. A pit of despair welled up from his extremities, and he felt that if he didn't yell he would choke on it.

'OUR FATHER, WHO ART IN HEAVEN –'

The children crawled and jerked and danced closer, closer.

'– HALLOWED BE THY NAME –'

The sun had turned somehow black, a seething mass high in the sky. All the flaming eyes of the dead children, dozens and dozens of the tiny lights, surged with invigorated glee.

'– THY KINGDOM COME, THY WILL BE DONE –'

The child who had climbed from his grave so close was now using Paolo's own cassock to pull himself along the length of the cardinal's body. His burning gaze was impossibly penetrating. Paolo felt his very bones shiver beneath those hard, bony fingers.

The boy pulled himself fully atop him, straddling the cardinal; worms and creepers and crawlers and black sludge rained down upon the pristine watered silk of Paolo's cassock. (Lorenzo had forgotten the embroidered *rochet*, and, for that matter, the *mozzetta*.) A dirty spike of a finger, the skin withered and barely clinging to the phalange, pressed itself against Paolo's trembling lips. That undercurrent of graveyard stench was suddenly overpowering.

'Daddy's gone,' the child's corpse seethed, grinning wickedly. 'His kingdom is right here.'

The other children loomed. From the ground, they appeared towering all of a sudden. Bigger than Paolo, bigger even than the statue of Saint Peter. The deep chasms in the earth yawned under the black sun. Paolo stared into the fiery sockets of the dead boy's eyes and he saw the truth.

A necropolis beneath the Piazza San Pietro! All this time? How did I not know?!

Children... scores of them... the desecrated, desiccated bodies of God's children, buried in secret in the one place they should be safe. It was wrong. It was *evil* –

'Evil, yes,' the child straddling him rasped, as if plucking the thought from Paolo's mind like a ripe fruit. 'Now you see the truth, old man. Now you see – '

Paolo's body jerked violently back, but the boy held firm, digging his exposed shin bones into the cardinal's sides. The movement was involuntary;

41

Paolo's mind rejected the rasping words to such a degree that it sent a fight-or-flight spark zipping through his every synapsis. The truth? What truth could this nightmarish creature be speaking of? Surely not –

But he knew. Paolo *knew*. And those smouldering fairy lights in this dead boy's eye sockets seemed to taunt him with that knowledge.

The truth. Yes, he saw the truth. The sweaty face of Lorenzo flashed in his mind's eye, and the way Cardinal Brizio lorded over the lad in such a domineering, possessive way. The Pope's burst heart in the privacy of his own papal suite. And something else... something Paolo had avoided thinking about for twelve long years.

It was back in his priesthood days. A historic cold front sent him shivering to the basement to kick the boiler back to life. But what he'd found – what he'd seen – even now, his mind refused to look at it straight on, instead choosing oblique angles that offered merciful denial.

The dead boy's dusty bone of a finger trailed up from Paolo's lips, dragging its jagged tip along his quivering cheek until it came to a rest at his temple. As if extracting the memory, the boy wheezed, 'Show

42

me.'

Paolo was thrown through time and space to that moment, that horrid moment. Stepping down into the frigid, dark basement of the church and seeing his colleague, in full clerical dress, and the altar boy. The altar boy, just barely at the age of reason, was bent over, his little hands spread across the cold boiler, his clothes bunched at his midriff to leave his bottom half exposed and glowing palely in the gloom. His little mousy face was screwed up in what Paolo knew was pain but his mind interpreted as prayer.

In the priest's hand was a miniature wooden cross, and it was inverted so that the long end could properly enter the child's rectum.

Paolo could see the blood, glinting crimson in the dark as it dripped down the boy's thighs.

He never did get the boiler running that day. Instead, the bishop made an urgent visit. Two weeks later, the priest was gone, shunted off to some diocese in South America. Paolo never thought of him again. Indeed, even as he saw the seven-year-old boy in mass each Sunday afterward, he remembered smiling and thinking, *The kingdom of heaven belongs to such as these!*

And here it was: the true kingdom of heaven, a secret grave of children, finally excavated by Saint

Peter himself so that they might seek their revenge. Surrounded overnight by a forest, come down upon Vatican Hill with the full force of God's righteous anger.

It was never the forest that was evil.

The evil was here all along.

And he, Paolo, was its cleric.

The dead boy's finger scraped across Paolo's temple until the little skeletal hand was cradling his head. It held him there, locked in a gaze with those shining flames for eyes surrounded by rotted flesh and writhing sludge.

'We've come to deliver you from evil, old man!'

The dead thing snaked his other hand behind Paolo's head to lock it in place. He brought his face closer, closer. Paolo could see maggots squirming in cracks in the boy's cheeks, like lively dimples. The mouth opened to a pool of black sludge and out tumbled a spongy slug of a tongue. Blue veins strained in an effort to push the tongue as far out as they could, until Paolo could see the root, glistening and bumpy like swollen braille. The smell was unbearable; the cardinal held his breath lest he gag.

The boy and his gaping mouth edged closer, closer.

Finally, the spell broke – Paolo unfroze. He could

not, *would* not, let this child kiss him, refused to join the likes of that long-ago priest in the basement. With a colossal effort, he threw off the corpse, and it was a shock how easily the arms around his neck broke, snapped like dusty kindling, a shock how weightless this skin-dressed skeleton was as it flew from him, knocking down the surrounding children as it landed.

Paolo scrambled back, unable to tear his eyes from the oncoming army of children. He was suddenly on his feet, his heart hammering, and then he was finally turned from that horrid sight and he was running. He'd lost one loafer but he dared not turn back.

He ran. He ran through the forest, once again letting the cloying dark beneath its boughs embrace him.

But he was not the only one running. He could hear, just beneath the thunderous roar of his own gasping breath – his own jackhammer for a heart – the scuffling and skitter of dozens of quick, spindly bodies chasing him through the forest. Children's gleeful whoops and hollers echoed in the strange air.

Paolo tried to put on a burst of speed, but already he could feel his body failing him. Healthy for his age, sure, but marathon sprinter he was not. He tried to calculate how far it was from the obelisk to the Basilica

San Pietro, but he knew it was pointless. It might as well be a million kilometres away. He would not escape. He would not warn the rest of the Vatican of the dangers of the forest.

God did not want him to escape its trees.

As if summoned by that thought, a new sound drowned out all others.

The sound of the forest itself.

Groaning, creaking boughs whipped through the viscous air as Paolo ran. An ocean's roar of leaves shushing against each other. Ripping tears from beneath, rumbling at his feet, as thick, roping roots yanked themselves free of the ground. Shards of the piazza's paving stones pelted through the air like mortars.

Paolo suddenly felt as if he were running through a tunnel that was under heavy artillery. He was never in the war – he'd always considered his trenches to be the pews – but now it was as though the tree trunks surrounding him were almost... shaking... twisting –

My God!

But his God did not answer. Or maybe He did, though without mercy, as the trees themselves ripped free of the earth and walked on tall roots like spider's legs. They walked and they herded him, making him turn this way and that, and with every turn a sense of overwhelming futility rose to clog his throat.

Before he could stop running, a tree branch whipped down and coiled around his torso. He screamed, and the sound was cut short as the branch constricted around him and he was made breathless. The ground zoomed away from him and his stomach tumbled as he soared into the air. The world became an incoherent mess of twisted trees and rubbery bark and horrible, syrupy sap.

The cardinal's body slammed against a hard, knotty surface. He was in too much pain to even cry out, but what would he say? He was alone. He was forsaken.

The forest floor was spread out before him, several metres below. The tree branch still held him, pinning him to its massive trunk. Two smaller branches whipped out of the darkness, wrapping around his wrists. Two more cinched his ankles.

Boom.

Through the commotion there was a thunderous rumble. The children's corpses, now capering at the tree's base, all stopped to listen.

Boom.

Paolo's heart stuttered. He knew that sound.

Boom.

All else grew still, and in that stillness each rumbling boom seemed to reverberate through the trees and the stones and the very air. When the source finally came into sight, Paolo's entire body shuddered in a horrified gasp.

'San Pietro,' he whispered.

It was the statue – the same statue he had watched methodically dismantle an entire platoon of Swiss Army guards. In just three more thunderous strides it stood before Paolo, who stared into those stone eyes and saw nothing.

Chittering from below, and swift, crawling movement at his feet. Several of the dead children skirted up the tree like spiders, laughing and jeering at him. He moaned when one began to lift his cassock.

He hung, immobile, as the children undressed him, casting his raiment to the forest floor. He did not try to protest or reason with them, instead closing his eyes and shuddering as their skeletal little fingers pinched at his wrinkly flesh.

He opened his eyes again, naked, hanging from the tree with his arms spread as wise as they would go. Saint Peter still stood there, staring, expressionless.

'Please...' Paolo's voice cracked in defeat. 'I'm asking you. God...'

Saint Peter stared silently back. Standing, he was at eye level with the hanging cardinal. He suddenly shot one stone hand out, and it connected with Paolo's left shinbone with a resounding *crack!*

Paolo screamed.

With each pummel of stone against bone, he screamed, but it had no effect on the statue. He continued his work until all that was left of Paolo's legs was loose, limply hanging skin. The bones were pulverized, shards sticking out at odd angles. He stared down at his ruined legs, drool dribbling down as he moaned hopelessly.

From out of the darkness came another moan, as if in reply.

He looked up and to the side of Saint Peter and saw for the first time that he was not alone in this crucifixion. The shifting, restless trees, still walking the forest floor on their stilt-like root systems, allowed just enough sunlight through the dense, dark air for him to make out his companions. At the sight of them, his surgeon's hands trembled.

Clergymen: bishops, cardinals, priests. Men of the cloth, all hanging from the wide, monstrous trees, their cloth stripped from their bodies and quietly moaning. In the shadowy depths of the forest the rows and rows of crucified bodies stretched beyond imagining.

So many, Paolo thought. *Surely not so many as this?*

But God did not answer. Paolo did not need Him to.

Yes, he thought. *These and so many more. All of us.*

Strung across the trunk closest to him was Cardinal Giuseppe Brizio. He moaned just as the others did, his head hanging down. Glassy eyes, shining in the darkness, stared down at his own nakedness. In the pale glow of his expanse of flesh was a splash of red. Paolo looked closer. The man had been disembowelled. Long ropes of intestine hung in loops from his spilled belly, glistening and twitching with life. Brizio sensed Paolo's eyes upon him and looked up, meeting his gaze.

We cannot let the Church fall in its darkest hour.

Those were among the last words Brizio had said to him, that morning that seemed now millennia away. At the time he had scoffed; now, he opened his heart. Falling was exactly what the Church would do. It had earned its place in this living Hell. They all had.

Darkest hour. Paolo thought of those young guards at the fountain, bleeding and torn limb from limb and yet still crying out for help. Still alive. Their darkest hour had stretched into eternity in the shade of this overnight forest.

A warmth spread across his belly, and he did not need to see to know: he could feel the slop of hot liquid, the slithering coils of intestine leaving his insides.

In that moment, Lorenzo's nervous face swam into his memory, and the words he had said to the lad before marching into his darkest hour.

Whatever happens in those trees? I am willing.

And he was.

He turned his gaze away from his fellow cardinal and he faced San Pietro, still standing before him, and he leaned his head back, letting gravity take his blood and his viscera and his body and hang it by his wrists.

His hands stilled.

OVER THE RIVER AND THROUGH THE WOODS

by Mocha Pennington

'Stop the car!' Kieran hollered, his fingers working eagerly at the zipper to the leather pouch in his lap. He pulled out the sleek camcorder with more force than needed, pressing down on the window switch. He grunted something inarticulate around an impatient breath as the window made its slow descent into the door.

The car came to a smooth halt.

'It's not like it's gonna go anywhere,' Trevor said from the driver's seat, humour in his voice. When Kieran pretended not to hear him, he smiled, shifting his gaze from the rearview mirror to the front door window.

'What is he looking at?' Harper asked beside Trevor

in the passenger's seat. She hoped the bleak nervousness in the question went undetected. Warily, she leaned a bit closer to see beyond Trevor's broad shoulder but could only make out those dense trees threaded with wisps of fog.

They were packed tightly together on either side of the thin strip of gravel road, as though protecting their depths from scrutiny. They stood impossibly tall, their immense height intimidating, hostile, in the way they lorded over their domain. Their thick, tortuous arms reached out to each other and joined hands, creating a cloak of foliage that filtered the afternoon sun in weak beams of dappled light along the road.

'That,' Trevor's voice pulled her from an unease that was dangerously close to fear. That fear had been ghosting around the outskirts of her subconscious since the sparse woodland had thickened, became impenetrable, seemingly alive. It was an insidious fear, all teeth and hunger, waiting for the perfect moment to devour her.

She followed Trevor's finger pressed against the glass. There, at the side of the road, stabbed into the moist earth, was a crucifix. It looked sad and out of place, a misfit compared to the giants that surrounded it. It may have once been elegant, baroque in design, though now its polished exterior had been stripped away, revealing dry, brittle wood; its beauty weatherworn, disfigured, as if by envious hands.

'Do you see that next to the crucifix?' Trevor asked, his nonchalance cracked by an excited lilt. He lifted his eyes from the window to turn to Kieran, ensuring he was heard. 'Zoom in on it,' Trevor instructed once Kieran had confirmed the sighting.

Harper was puzzled for a moment, but then she too saw it. Cast off a foot or so from the crucifix was a bouquet of what she assumed once were flowers. Muddy, water damaged cellophane barely clung around the withered corpses of unidentifiable flowers. Fleetingly, she wondered: if she held those colourless petals in her hands, would they turn to mush or crumple into dust?

'That's creepy,' Rosé stated, her voice like a bored shrug. She returned her eyes to her phone, slender fingers roaming across the screen.

A dismissal.

Harper lingered on her for a bit longer, still wondering why exactly she was here with them. It wasn't like the two were close or even friends for that matter. They exchanged glib niceties, simply tolerating each other for the sake of Trevor and Kieran, which happened to be just about all they had in common.

'Rosé's coming with us,' Trevor had told Harper last night, finality in his tone, a brick wall with no room for debate.

As if she would attempt to.

With her eyes lowered, Rosé's lashes seemed to eat up half her face. They were long and thick, obviously fake, giving the impression of the fluttering wings of a butterfly. Her hair was platinum blonde, tinged the faintest hue of pink; half an inch of dark roots peeked from the part, as if to remind you, if you couldn't already tell, that the colour was the result of an expensive trip to the salon.

When she caught Harper staring at her, she reacted in a bright smile rather than a perturbed frown. Maintaining her smile, she nudged her head in Kieran's direction and gave her green eyes a playful toss heavenward. *Our men care about their documentaries more than us, am I right?* That eye roll seemed to say.

Harper returned the smile, hers not as bright and definitely not as confident. She broke eye contact, turning back onto the macabre still life outside the humming vehicle. She was wondering why they stopped to film such a depressing visual and what it had to do with the subject of their current documentary, when Kieran spoke:

'Should I get out for some close ups? I want to get enough footage where we can insert a voiceover, telling the story without using any b-roll.'

Harper cocked her head, unsure if she had heard correctly. She didn't like the feeling that pierced through her flesh, flickering in the pit of her stomach like the struggling wings of a bird before claimed by Death. That feeling made itself physical, creasing at her brow, suspicion with anger shimmering just beneath.

'What story?' She asked, hoping she was able to keep the heated emotions from her voice.

Trevor visibly stiffened at the question. Slowly, he began to turn to her, his expression one of guilt masquerading as casualness, his eyes deep pools of calculation. He was going to lie to her, she knew, or at the very least, omit details of the truth.

'There was a car accident here,' Kieran said. He was training his camcorder on the crucifix, his voice a distracted drawl. 'A therapist and his family. He swerved off the road somehow, ended up killing his son, wife, and their unborn child. Someone erected that crucifix and began bringing bouquets to it once or twice a month.

'It's widely believed their deaths messed with the doctor's head. A year later, on the exact day of the accident, he just –' Kieran shrugged '– snapped. He brought a patient and an orderly out in these woods under false pretences. The orderly was found dead, multiple gunshot wounds to the head; completely mutilated. The therapist and patient were never seen again. The bouquets stopped showing up after that.'

A shadow of annoyance passed over Trevor's features but quickly dissipated when he realised that Harper was watching him. He mustered up a smile that had threat at its edges.

Her fingers went to the healing bruise at her ribs. She added pressure to it, biting against the swell of pain. She pressed into that tender patch once more, just as a reminder.

Trevor began to tell her about another incident that involved a social media influencer who was kidnapped and held hostage in a cabin somewhere in these woods, but her thoughts drifted.

...in these woods under false pretences.

Her mind kept circling back to those words. False pretences. Wasn't that why she agreed to have this entire experience filmed?

She suddenly felt stupid, naïve. A new hatred for Trevor spread through her like a stealthy, black cancer, threatening to hollow her out until she was nothing more than the flaccid flesh of a young woman, animated by rancour.

Harper's parents made it no secret that she had been adopted, and even if they wanted to, anyone with a pair of working eyes could tell they did not don the same genetic makeup. Both her parents were tall and pale, their features heavily dredged from northern European blood. Harper was short, her skin a warm fawn that was forever golden, even in the heart of winter; her glossy, raven curls tumbled passed her shoulders, looping in a silky S pattern.

She had always known African blood ran through her, but how deep that blood ran, she was unsure. There weren't any records that connected her to her birth parents. She had been fresh out the womb when she was discovered outside the doors to a police station, as if she were a donation box, crammed with random, unusable implements, too worthless to be bothered with direct contact.

The thought of wanting to find her birth parents never entered her mind, but she was always curious about her genes. As a child, she would often look over a world map, trying to piece together potential countries that gave her the features that would later be described as "exotic".

Two months ago, her curiosity was put to rest after submitting a DNA swab to a website that boasted on tracking down one's ancestry. She wasn't at all surprised when finding out good portion of her DNA was traced back to Africa. The rest was found in small European villages sparkled around The Netherlands and Great Britain. What she didn't plan on discovering was the name and email address of a relative who didn't live too far from her.

When she first told Trevor she was able to track down a blood relative from a genetic test, he was mildly interested. He maintained an encouraging smile, weighed down with boredom, as she told him about how her relative put her in contact with her birth parents. His interest only piqued when she revealed that her birth parents lived in Mystic Hills, a small town in Georgia.

Over the course of two weeks, Trevor persisted on Harper meeting her birth parents. What started as a gentle suggestion turned into an almost furious demand. 'This will be good for you,' he had reasoned in a smile blistering under the heat of desperation. It had been something like a mantra of his, spoken so many times the words wormed themselves into her head, haunted her dreams until she believed them to be true.

She should have known Trevor's interest in her unwanted reunion with her birth parents was completely selfish when he offered to film it.

Trevor was speaking now – something about the woods and another disappearance.

'How far away did all this happen?' Rosé asked when he had finished, a thread of dismay twisting itself into her words. She was facing the car window, watching the woods carefully, her gaze laden with dark curiosity, as though expecting at any moment to be seized from the car by a skeletal branch from the woods.

Does she feel it too? Harper wondered.

She felt like a thousand eyes glared from the

woods. The woods themselves appeared to be encroaching, waiting for the precise moment that her guard was down to invade.

Harper had thought it was the nerves from the impending meeting with her birth parents that squeezed at her insides, but she now knew that something about those woods – or what lay cloaked in their darkness – provoked thrusting waves of trepidation to wash over her.

Kieran swerved the camcorder on Harper. 'You're about twenty minutes away from meeting your biological parents,' he said melodramatically, using his best Lester Holt impersonation, 'how are you feeling?'

'I... umm... I... I'm unsure,' she stammered. It wasn't the complete truth. She was terrified, but her birth parents had nothing to do with that.

'Come on, babe,' Trevor said. He placed a seemingly encouraging hand on her arm. She had the urge to push it off, as though a large, malformed insect had crawled onto her. 'Give a little more than that.' He gave her arm a squeeze, his fingernails biting into her like vampiric teeth, eager for its first taste of blood.

He smiled at her, a wolf in sheep's clothing. What

was it she ever saw in him?

She turned back to Kieran and forced brightness in her voice. 'I'm unsure how to feel. I'm about to meet people who I know nothing of. I guess –'

As she shifted her eyes to the car window to gather her thoughts, her voice dried up and stuck to her throat. She saw the silhouette of something moving quickly behind the dense, milky fog suspended in the air like a diaphanous curtain.

It was a tall, slender figure – of what? She wasn't positive. It was hunched over, gliding on beastly hind legs. Its arms were abnormally long, held up to its narrow chest like those belonging to a praying mantis. It didn't run but *galloped* out of her vision just as sudden as it entered it.

She must have made some sort of startled sound. Concern folded into the features of the three in the car with her. They brought their attention to where she stared, uncertainty stiffening their movements.

Their taut muscles slackened like a sigh of relief when nothing could be found besides an endless sea of towering, decrepit trees.

'I thought I saw something,' she told them, not wanting to come off as defensive but knowing she had.

The camcorder's lens scrutinized her like a

judgmental eye.

From her peripheral, she could have sworn she saw Trevor at war with a smile struggling to be seen.

'It was those fucking stories,' Rosé spoke up, looking to Harper. 'They freaked you out so much, they had you seeing things.' She nodded her head, as if willing Harper to agree. Her gaze then swept between Kieran and Trevor as she went on, 'I know you two assholes love this creepy shit for your little YouTube documentaries, but could you lay off with the messed-up stories? It already looks like we're on the set of *Wrong Turn: Part 23*.'

'Hey!' Kieran called out, lowering the camcorder in feigned outrage. 'The revenue from our little YouTube documentaries bought you that duffle bag you call a purse.'

Rosé snatched the immense, monogram-covered leather bag from her side and hugged it protectively to her chest, her face imbued with humour. Kieran playfully poked her in the side, causing her to squirm in a fit of giggles.

Harper turned from the backseat and stared forward. She pretended what Rosé had said was true. Those stories had somehow sent her imagination into overdrive. But if that were the case, why could she sense something watching her from the woods?

She shook the thought away and revisited a question that had often stalked her: What if she had chosen Kieran over Trevor?

She had met the pair last year while out for a drink following a stressful day at her father's dental office where she worked as a receptionist.

She was halfway finished with her second whiskey and Pepsi (she never liked Coke) when the two sat near her at the bar. Within five minutes of small talk, the two were in an obvious competition for her attention, talking over each other while they zealously discussed details of the documentaries they made on haunted locations. They fancied themselves as amateur paranormal investigators.

She was instantly attracted to Kieran. She adored his sense of humour, the way his hazel eyes bore into her as she spoke, devouring her every word, and the dimples dotting his walnut-coloured skin when he smiled.

With his blond hair and blue eyes, Trevor had an All-American boy exterior, yet there was a brooding quality beneath its surface – a mysterious something that drew her in, asking of her to peel back his layers and find what dwelled at his core.

Six months into their relationship, Harper found each layer she folded back was more tarnished than the last until she was digging through black globs of fetid decay. She never reached his core, too frightened to find what festered there.

She had come to the realization that she should have chosen Kieran too late. He had moved on.

When Kieran proudly introduced her to Rosé, it took every bit of her to choke back her jealousy and force what she hoped was the resemblance of a smile onto her face as she shook her hand.

Wasn't it Rosé who suggested she look into the website that traced DNA?

Trevor started his car and placed his hand on her thigh. 'Are you okay?' he asked when their eyes met. Though his words were hollow and artificial, the truth wanted to be spoken. It lunged itself at her lips like a turbulent river to a stubborn dam. But she forsook the truth, because once birthed, it would be real. She wasn't okay and hadn't been since having that first and only conversation with those strangers who created, incubated then abandoned her.

Fear had clung to her since that day, a tumour growing inside her, contaminating her cells, which wouldn't be satisfied until it wholly became her; fear that was an ever-present shadow, looming just out of reach. Harper felt that fear near a fever-pitch when they began their journey to meet those two strangers with the withering, odd voices who were suspiciously eager to meet her.

'I'm fine,' she said, flat and cold. She brushed his large hand off her thigh. His eyes rested on her, their intensity a searing blade, cauterizing as it slid effortlessly through her. She kept her eyes downward, as if she were a student chastised by a hated teacher. She didn't know which set of eyes she feared more: The ones inside the car or the ones outside of it.

Gravel crunched under the car's weight as it moved down a road that grew thinner with distance. The trees inched their way closer, their branches like salivating tongues, yearning for just a taste of its meal. The further they journeyed, the darker their surroundings became, the shadows bleeding together to create the fallacy of midnight amid a cold winter. The illusion was punctured sporadically by defiant shafts of sunlight, leaking through a verdure canopy in the palest shades of yellow.

The robotic voice of the GPS announced their destination was on the left. Trevor slowly made the turn, parting through a condensed veil of fog. They were greeted by a long stretch of a pathway leading to a small clearing dotted erratically with what seemed to be vehicles. Amongst the throng of vehicles was a house. Even through the great distance, it was apparent the house had seen better days.

'Nervous?' Rosé asked. Her voice was husky, almost sexual; the tone in it suggested they were former lovers, sharing an intimate joke.

Harper met her gaze in the side mirror. Her skin prickled as a dank chill penetrated her, a chill that had nothing to do with the weather.

Rosé's face was emotionless, a ball of clay waiting to be given life. She had always had a peculiar glow about her, as if she went about her days with a perfect blurring filter hovering over her. That filter had now slipped, revealing dull skin, each imperfection made harsher, as though seen through a magnifying glass. A smirk snaked across Rosé's face, further marring her beauty, darkening her eyes to an ominous obsidian. One of her strip lashes had come unbonded. It remained stuck to her eyelid for a moment then tumbled down her face. Rosé didn't seem bothered by it.

'Umm...' Kieran began, breaking Harper's spell, 'I don't think they're animal lovers.' Something close to – but not quite – panic peeked through the humour in his words.

Harper turned in her seat. Kieran was looking out the window through the lens of his camcorder. She muffled a gasp with a quaking hand.

Piled along the treeline were animal carcasses, most of which were dismembered. The severed heads of deer and elk dangled from low tree branches, blood and tissue dried to a black crust around jagged necklines that looked like they had been torn from their bodies rather than cut. Limbs and hooves, some with clinging ligaments that looked like stretched Laffy-Taffy, also appeared to have been ripped from their bodies and carelessly discarded.

Most of the limbless torsos were shattered open with bloodied entrails ballooning from the fractures. The few animal corpses that were still intact had large chunks missing from them, as if a great beast had taken a sample bite but decided it wasn't to its liking.

The pieces littered the blood-darkened ground in various stages of decay, a never-ending buffet for the swarm of insects to feast upon.

'Fuck,' Trevor breathed. If he were scared, then it was hidden beneath a façade of calm. He lifted his eyes to the rearview mirror. The emotion twisting into his handsome features was pure astonishment in the form of a smile. 'Now *that* you can get some close-ups of!' He then laughed, humour and disgust commingled into a thin, strained sound. He tossed a glance at Harper and winked, inviting her in on a joke she didn't understand.

For a horrible moment, she thought she was going to lose it. She could see herself taking a fistful of Trevor's perfectly groomed hair and sending his face into the steering wheel until his skull shattered, leaving a concaved, gelatinous mess where his face had once been.

Her fingers twitched, the urge to play out that fantasy almost a desperate plea that made her entire body ache. She folded her hands in her lap, not trusting them to act out on their own accord.

'There has to be hundreds of them,' Kieran marvelled, more to himself than to anyone. His voice pulled her attention back to the side mirror.

Her eyes rested on Rosé, who was watching the horrors outside scroll past the car. There was something awful about her face – something that sent the tip of a gelid blade dragging down the length of her spine. A hunger emanated from her, a raw, animalistic hunger that dehumanized her features, making her look wild, feral.

Rosé gingerly ran her fingers down the window; a dark tongue slithered from her dry, cracked lips, wetting them.

'You have arrived at your destination,' the GPS announced, the cheery note in its voice a contradiction to their dismal surroundings.

The clearing before them was a vehicle graveyard. Dissected cars and trucks were scattered across yellowed grass, their frames rusted and contorted, their windows pebbled on their moss-blighted seats. The house at the centre was almost lost in the chaotic labyrinth of steel and neglect.

The house was a single-story structure that barely clung to the life it had left. The house spoke of a life that began with defective materials, constructed by lazy, inexperienced hands; the result of a half-thought idea conjured by an unimaginative mind. Its paint was chipped and discoloured, the wood beneath eroded, the evidence of its abusive relationship with the elements. Vines crawled up its sides like bandages, trying to keep it from collapsing into the devastation it beseeched for.

Harper freed herself from the car and stood under the bright afternoon sun. They had spent so long traveling through an eerie darkness fashioned by trees, she had forgotten it was a cloudless summer day.

'What's going through your mind right now?' Kieran asked. She didn't need to turn around to confirm he was standing behind the probing eye of the camcorder.

I feel like this is a setup, she wanted to answer. Instead, she held her tongue and headed toward the sagging porch.

Do you ever feel like you don't belong? It was Rosé's voice she heard. Out of the whirlwind of screaming thoughts flowing through her mind like a shaken snow globe, it was the loudest one.

Rosé had asked her that question the first time they met after Harper had told her she was adopted. The question had been asked by many different people in various different ways. She was accustomed to the question, expected it. She opened her mouth to deliver the line she had perfected over the years, but her voice faltered, her perfect lie unable to be summoned. There had been something *knowing* in Rosé's eyes that murdered the lie on her tongue and extracted the truth.

I never felt like I belonged, she had answered. It was a

72

truth she never wanted to drag out from the shadows and force into the light. It wasn't just her parents who she didn't feel a part of, it was everyone she met. She had always felt like an outsider, an imposter tiptoeing through someone else's life. She thought of herself to be the greatest actress who could portray any role given to her.

Rosé had smiled at that, the smile never reaching her obsidian-colored eyes (weren't her eyes green?). *That's because you don't*, Rosé said.

Harper turned to Rosé now. Had she grown taller? She walked abreast to Kieran, matching his six-foot-three height. Her skin had a greyish tint to it, and it looked thicker too, drier, like desiccated earth. That horrible skin looked as if it would split open if she were to so much as stretch.

Rosé caught her staring and grinned. It was an awful grin. It was too wide, the corners reaching her ears; the teeth lining her gums were the monstrous teeth of a shark.

Harper faced forward, telling herself she was seeing things, that her mind was playing cruel tricks on her. The most believable lies are the ones people tell themselves.

Once on the porch, she paused, fear prickling over

her skin. She noticed the silence for the first time. It wasn't just any silence, but a complete absence of sound, as though Mother Nature had hit the mute button on the world.

Slowly, she turned to the left and then the right, taking in her surroundings. No birds flew aloft; the leaves to those impossibly tall trees did not stir; the wildlife concealed behind the thick curtain of fog did not call out to each other.

That uncanny silence deepened her fear, rooting it to her bone marrow. It was a preamble, that silence was, foreshadowing horrors yet unseen. A lethargic deluge of fog began to spill from the woods, swallowing all in its path.

Harper backed away from the front door, shaking her head as if someone had made an accusation she vehemently denied.

'Goddamn it, Harper. Knock on the fucking door,' Trevor said through clenched teeth. His mask had slipped, revealing the hateful man she has grown to despise. He was a man with little patience and a tongue that had left bruises lasting longer than his hands ever could.

Kieran was a few feet behind him, watching the scene unfold behind the lens of his camcorder. Was he oblivious to the sugarcoated persona Trevor presented to the world, or was he a wilful accomplice?

Rosé was strayed off from the three, a shadow now, evanescing in the thickening fog.

'You're ruining this documentary for us!' Trevor hissed at her ear as he brushed passed her. He marched to the front door and pounded his fist on it.

Every fibre in Harper screamed for her to run, yet morbid curiosity kept her in place.

There was movement from inside the belly of that crumbling house. Rapid footfalls. No... *stomps*, like the roll of thunder. They could be felt in the floorboards of the porch, seen rippling in the dusty glass in the brittle window frames. Just as Harper took a step backward, something thrust itself into the door. Dust belched in a cloud from the impact; the wood crackled, leaving a gash in the door that emanated a cold breath that smelt of age and rot.

Another set of stomps sounded from inside the house. They were heavier than their predecessor, more frantic. A dreadful desperation could be felt in their rapid gait, a primal hunger.

Harper was at the bottom of the steps when the front door exploded open. Wood fragments flung past her, struck her in the shoulders and back. She picked up speed at the sound of low growls, emitting from something large and inhuman.

She heard Trevor scream in a terror so strong it gripped his mind and squeezed, his brains oozing between terror's fingers. His screams rose an octave or two. He was in blinding torment. His screams turned wet, guttural, and then nonexistent.

As she put more distance between she and that house, she could still hear the faint song of wet bone snapping and skin tearing, playing as a soundtrack to the cruel stillness of the day – a symphony of blood and flesh for her to move in a danse macabre as she neared an uncertain future.

Harper underestimated the density of the fog. Knowing he kept a spare key under the floor mat in the footwell, she thought she could make it to Trevor's car and rid herself of this terrible town. She got confused somewhere. Being amid the fog was like being caught inside a blizzard. Her vision was compromised by stirring walls of grey.

All the dark shapes of the cars in the yard looked the same until they loomed before her, revealing themselves to be wrecked and useless, a wicked taunt.

She knew she should have turned around when she found herself at the mouth of the woods, but she somehow felt she'd be safer enveloped in them.

Her surmise was correct upon entering them. An odd relief flooded through her, warming the pit of her stomach, nestling there. The fog was much thinner in the woods too. She was able to amble through them surefootedly.

The temperature was several degrees colder, causing a persistent chill to press against her. The sun wasn't welcome there; not even a rebellious, wayward beam was able to penetrate the tree's shroud. A pall of night painted the woodland in deep, grim hues.

She knew animals treaded in these woods, but they were miles away now. Something has scared them off. Yes, they were afraid; she could smell fear's sour scent in the air. She could also smell something else too. Something sweet.

She shoved the other scents polluting the air aside, isolating that sweet smell. She inhaled deeply. Her mouth watered and her stomach rumbled.

Before she knew what she was doing, she was pursuing the scent. Harper weaved her way through trees and low-hanging branches, surprising herself by how quick and graceful she moved. As she closed in on that fragrance, she realized it was something she had smelt many times before.

She came upon the scent to find Kieran sitting against a tree trunk, his sweat-sheeted face contorted in a mask of agony. The hem of his pant leg was soaked in dark blood: the culprit of the sweet smell.

'Oh, my God! Harper!' He called out in a voice taunt in pain. 'I-I-I'm sorry. I shouldn't have left everyone,' he said sheepishly, his head in a shameful bow. 'Whatever was inside that house freaked me out, and I took off. I should've known not to come here, I just –'

His speech broke when he followed her gaze to his leg.

'I cut it on a piece of glass or something.' He shrugged. 'Hell, if I know,' he said in a puff of humourless laughter.

Why did she want to lick his wound, wring his pant leg in her mouth? Why wasn't she sickened by the visual of biting into him, savouring the taste of his raw flesh?

He continued when she made no move to reply. 'It was so stupid to come here. Trevor and I knew this place was fucked, but didn't think it was *this* fucked.' He slowly shook his head. 'Trevor thought reuniting you with your birth parents was a perfect angle for a three-part docuseries,' he gestured to the battered camcorder at his side. 'Trevor and I weren't supposed to tell you, but Rosé said she spent a few summers here to stay with her grandparents. She was going to show us all the creepy places here.'

'Rosé's been here?'

He confirmed in a weak nod. 'Is she okay, do you know? What about Trevor?'

'Trevor is dead,' she told him. A smile touched her lips. Speaking those words aloud made her happy. She was glad he was dead; her only regret was not being able to see the life slowly depart from his eyes. 'I don't know where Rosé is.'

That wasn't entirely true, was it? If she wanted to, she could easily track her location just as easily as she found Kieran. She was somewhere in these woods, she knew that, and close. Harper could sense her presence. It was a faint sensation, like the nearly-there feeling of someone running their fingertips ever-so-gently down her back.

She shifted her eyes from Kieran to the empty space at the side of the tree. A few heartbeats later, Rosé appeared. She stood behind a thin veil of fog. Her features were just visible, yet their details were obscured.

She had shed herself of society's disguise to show her true self. Her tall, slender body was made up of all sharp angles and jagged points, caught in some horrid place between human and monster. Stringy, lank hair formed around a face that was like puckered leather. Her too-long fingers were like blades and just as dangerous.

Harper thought of Freddy Krueger and tried not to laugh. Was she going mad?

'It was rude of you to leave in the middle of dinner,' Rosé said; there was a huskiness to her voice, as if she chewed and swallowed glass, 'and without bidding your parents a goodbye.' Something like a smirk cut into her face from ear to ear.

'Don't move,' Harper told Kieran when noticing him struggling to his feet at the sound of Rosé's voice. The muted reek of fear emanated from Kieran in delicate coils. His body knew to be scared, but his mind wasn't sure of what.

'Yeah, Kieran, stay where you are. I'll be *mortified* if you see me without my makeup on.' Rosé deadpanned.

'Those...*things* are my parents?' Harper asked.

'Well, that's not a very polite word to describe them, now is it? They went to great lengths to arrange your homecoming.'

'How is that possible? I don't understand.'

'You understand a lot more than you care to admit to yourself. We would be happy to fill you in on everything else.'

That was when Harper felt them, hundreds of eyes watching from the woods. They were alert, the watchers behind those eyes were, their demeanour even, but one that could turn hostile at a moment's notice. All it took was a single command.

'You're right to be apprehensive of us,' Rosé said, perhaps noticing uncertainty shape itself into Harper's face, or smelling it radiate from her pores. 'We can destroy you, but we don't want to. You're one of us. You sense it, don't you? You belong here.'

Harper couldn't deny she felt comfortable here in these woods, among its occupants. It was a sense she never experienced before; it was welcoming, like an embrace from a loved one.

'Join us,' Rosé continued, her voice lower, kinder. 'We just need to dispose of the evidence.' Her eyes moved down to Kieran, who sat with his knees pulled to his chest, his body trembling.

Panic bloomed in Harper's chest. 'No!' she cried out, louder than expected. The watcher's eyes narrowed, their legs bent slightly, ready to pounce if needed. 'He leaves here unharmed. It's all I ask for.'

Rosé thought about that for a moment, then shrugged. 'Very well.'

Harper went to Kieran and kneeled before him. She managed to stifle a gasp after placing her hand on his shoulder. Her skin was deeply textured and an ashy color. It looked like it was lifting from its bone, ready to split open. Her fingers were elongated; her fingernails didn't look like nails, but shards of glass stuffed into the nailbeds.

When did this metamorphosis commence? Had it been when she entered the woods, or had it always rested beneath her skin, dormant, waiting to be stirred awake?

'There's a car key under the floor mat,' she told him. 'Get out of here.'

She wanted to say more, tell him that she wished she chose him over Trevor. She wanted to kiss him goodbye yet was hindered by the possibility that he would shove her away, sheer disgust carving itself into his face by what her former self was succumbing to.

She watched him limp away and vanish into the fog before rising to her feet.

The things that emerged from the fog were

hideous, misshapen monstrosities. They crowded around her, whispering among themselves in a language that was completely alien to her. The longer she listened, however, she was able to catch fragments she could decipher until their secret language of grunts and barks made sense.

For the first time in her life, she was at peace.

FURRY SKINS

by L. Pine

Shaw let out a triumphant whoop as the last echoes of gunshot faded into the trees. He marched over with long, confident strides to where the beast lay, but still displayed the caution that came with experience. You always had to be just a little careful making sure things of that size were actually dead, and not just stunned. But he had his skill to count on, and the bullet had hit straight through the skull, leaving it lifeless by the riverbank with its muzzle lolling in the mud, black eyes wide open and glassy and its limbs buckled beneath it at odd angles.

Shaw gave another exhilarated laugh, still rushing from the high of adrenaline and gunfire. He prodded the carcass with the tip of his steel-toed boot, before giving it a rougher nudge with the barrel of his gun for good measure. 'That's gonna be ten thousand bucks for me! Now,' he squatted down on the bank and peered closely at his kill, scratching at the black stubble on his neck. 'Just what the hell are you?'

He'd never seen anything like it before in his entire profession as a hunter and now that the thrill of the hunt was over, he could allow himself to be curious. It looked like a weasel – if a weasel could grow to the size of a bear. Bigger, even. The head wasn't quite the right shape, the muzzle was too long, the head too bullet-shaped. The hind legs were short and beast-like, but there was something off about the front limbs. They were way too long, and too skinny.

Too human.

They looked less like forelegs and more like arms, and that thought was off-putting to Shaw. The fur ended at the wrists; the paws just bare pink flesh, if they could be called paws. Really, they looked like hands, as big as Shaw's torso, each with five long fingers, so thin the knuckles stood out, round and knobbly and tipped with a sleek, black talon, as long as a hunting knife. It was not something he'd relish facing off against.

'Well, good thing I'm smarter than you, ain't it?' Shaw sneered, grasping the weasel-shaped abomination by the ear, lifting its head and forcing its mouth open to examine the teeth. They were all long and pearly, sharp as razors. He let the head fall back against the bank, running a hand through its pelt. That was the best part of all. The whole body was covered in thick, snowy white fur, soft and downy to the touch.

Shaw whistled. 'That'll fetch a price too. What do you think? Reckon he'll let me do what I want with your pieces if I barter with him?'

Laughing again, Shaw straightened up and started preparing the carcass for the haul back to his truck, securing it with harnesses and chatting mockingly to it all the while. He was in an exceptionally good mood. This was possibly the easiest hunt of his career, and would be the best paying one too. The man who owned the property had offered him ten thousand dollars – ten thousand! – and it hadn't taken him more than an hour of tracking.

He'd only been scouting for trails that he could leave traps on, and the beast had practically dropped into his lap. It had simply arrived, lumbering out into the open without so much as a look or cautious sniff around, entirely focused on getting a drink of water from the riverbank, making itself a perfect target.

It hadn't even heard the click of the safety.

It had been completely oblivious to the danger.

Shaw laughed again as he thought about it. It almost seemed like robbery to ask for the full ten thousand with how easy this had been, but he wasn't stupid enough to cut the fee. He'd never get that kind of money for such an easy job ever again, and he'd take the blessing offered him.

Whatever this thing was, or how it had gotten there, wasn't something he cared about. An animal was an animal, and though Shaw was partial to a challenge on occasion, they were all just meat and skins to him in the end.

He'd parked his truck uphill at the mouth of the woods where the river was no longer at ground level, but at the bottom of a steep bluff several yards high. This made hauling the carcass a task, but Shaw was in too good a mood to complain. Time hauling was time spent daydreaming about his plans for the money. Such thoughts made the work lighter, so in no time at all he had reached his truck.

He was so engrossed in the hot, sweaty work of dragging the carcass onto the pickup bed and securing it, that a distant sound almost didn't catch his attention.

Shaw paused, wiping his sweaty mullet out of his face and glaring into the trees. Instinct kept him alert, remaining still and quiet as he waited to hear it again, so that he might be able to define it.

And he did hear it. A soft, guttural growl somewhere not too far off.

Shaw cast a glance down at his prize, frowning. The big white creature's head had been bent and cocked to fit inside the truck bed, and it stared up at him with one filmy black eyeball, its mouth a grimace of death.

Quite obviously not the source. As if to confirm this, a fly crawled over the snout, pausing to rub its feet together.

Shaw vaulted over the side of the truck, unstrapping his shotgun from his shoulders and tentatively readying it against his shoulder. He swiveled his head, dark eyes darting back and forth as he scanned the clearing for any signs of motion in the trees. It wasn't unusual for an opportunistic predator to smell the blood from a hunt and take their chances tracking it to the source. The likelihood that he was in any danger was slim, but the weird look of the beast he'd killed was enough to make him suspicious of what was out there.

But when time passed without another odd sound he lowered his firearm with a snort.

'I ain't got time to be jumping at shadows,' he muttered. He was about to hitch his gun over his shoulder and jump onto the bed again, when the sound of bark scraping and twigs snapping made him jerk back around.

For a second he didn't see anything – but then he caught the movement, the shift of fur and muscles against the trunk of a tree.

He hadn't noticed it before, its brown fur blended with the bark, but he couldn't believe he could miss a pair of eyes like that, huge and round, as big as dinner plates – bigger! It had been perched in the branches above his line of sight, its forelegs gripping the trunk as it slowly eased its way down the tree with all the lithe danger of a wild cat.

It didn't look the same as the dead creature in Shaw's pickup but it was just as absurd, resembling a cross between a long eared bat and one of those weird things he'd seen in a national geographic – a bush baby, they'd called it. It was smaller, about half the size of the other beast and despite its bat-like look, it had no wings, but it had the same off-putting human-looking arms and hands, fingers equipped with talons. Its rounded head had a wide mouth that stretched almost all the way to its pointed, bat-like ears which flattened against its head as it hissed at him, revealing rows of pearly, razor sharp teeth. The glinting eyes narrowed, jaws pulling back into a snarl, then it opened its mouth and emitted a ghastly, furious shriek, muscles tensing to spring.

He slung his shotgun back into place, but wasn't quick enough to aim in time. The beast propelled itself off the tree, the slug missing it by seconds, ricocheting in a shower of bark, the deafening sound of the shot ringing through the woods. Shaw was knocked onto his back and slung across the forest floor with a single swipe from a huge set of claws. It tore through his clothes and only just scraped his flesh. He scrambled to get to his feet, bellowing a slew of swearwords in his panic and rage.

The beast crouched low to the ground mere feet from him, muscles tensing for another lunge. It gave a high-pitched screech that ended in a low, growling hiss.

Shaw knew he had no chance without distance.

Gripping the shotgun in both hands, he struck out, clubbing the creature in the face with the butt right above its huge left eye. It drew back with a scream of pain, and Shaw was on his feet, running.

He could hear it coming after him, the scratching of bark and rustling of leaves letting him know it was leaping from tree to tree, ready to drop on top of him.

He reached the edge of the steep drop, the river chuckling below him. Forced to go no further, he turned on his heel, cocking and gripping the shotgun with white knuckles and tensed shoulders as he scanned the treetops. He heaved for breath, letting out a feral growl of his own.

'Where are you?!' he spat out, voice ringing back to him. 'Come and get me!'

He'd barely let the words out when a huge, furry body pounced from the underbrush in a wild flurry of leaves and dirt.

Shaw yelled, adjusting his aim and firing, but again the creature was too fast for him, the bullet only sending up a blast of earth into his eyes and nose. Another blow from a hefty, clawed hand as he backed up to avoid teeth, claws, and dirt knocked him off balance. He lost his footing with a howl of surprise, plummeting into the river with stomach-dropping speed as the ground vanished from beneath him.

The cold water shocked the breath out of him, but he had enough forethought to sling his shotgun over his shoulder, arms and legs flailing as he fought the current.

His head breached the surface long enough to see the beast glaring down at him from the top of the bluff, before it turned away, and the water dragged Shaw under again.

Shaw lay spread eagled against a flat, mossy boulder, soaked through and seething.

His orange down vest had worked as something of a buoy against the river, and being an outdoorsman made him a strong swimmer. However, he'd been carried a good distance before he'd managed to drag himself to dry land, and he wasn't sure exactly how far out he was.

The man who'd hired him hadn't bothered to mention that there were two of the big ugly freaks out here in the woods. Hell, Shaw would guess that he didn't have any idea what was out here at all! But what could you expect from someone with enough money to pay ten thousand dollars a hide? He had plenty of cash to pay some low class sap to get killed so he could avoid the risk himself.

Shaw rubbed the right side of his jaw, wincing. He'd hit his face against a rock when he'd fought with the current, and the spot was beginning to swell. He stuck a grimy finger into his mouth, massaging his swelling gums and feeling each yellowed, crooked tooth to check if any were loose.

Aside from the pain, he hadn't taken any real damage.

But his pride was a different matter.

He forced a shaking hand into a soaked pocket of his pants, searching for his can of dip, and swore when he remembered that he'd left it on his front seat.

He had no doubt that the carcass was being made into a feast and would be damaged beyond selling by the time he got back to his truck. If he wanted his payout, he'd have to get back fast.

He sat up, rage giving him new energy. Just let the little slimeball try and not pay him after this!

Taking action, Shaw slung his shotgun from his shoulder and examined it, before cursing and putting himself to the task of dismantling and cleaning the water out. He tore off his vest, red flannel, boots, and socks, leaving only his camouflage pants, squeezing and shaking out the water from everything while he let his gun dry, staying alert for any suspicious sounds or movement.

The shotgun shells might be damaged, so he couldn't rely on firing it just yet anyway, and aside from the hunting knife firmly clipped to his belt, he was unarmed and vulnerable. It was a feeling he hated on principle.

His thoughts were occupied on vengeful retribution against his client, and the bitch that had attacked him. He was dead convinced it was a female, because no male animal would attack with such vindictive spite and ferocity. No, it was a lady beast alright, no doubt about it.

The client, a man by the name of Joseph Boyle, had not impressed Shaw, and he could tell that the feeling was mutual. When Shaw had driven onto Boyle's expensively landscaped property in his beat-up truck, blaring country music out of his speakers with the window open, wearing his grungiest (but best) hunting clothes, Mr. Boyle had made a polite effort to mask his disdain.

'Frank Shaw, I presume?' he'd asked, folding his hands behind his back without offering a handshake. Which was fine, because Shaw wouldn't have given him one if he had. Boyle was a short, pudgy, overdressed man that Shaw towered over by a good length. You could tell at a glance that he was the type who gave limp handshakes.

Shaw spat a squirt of dip onto the manicured lawn, grinning as he saw Mr. Boyle flinch. 'What gave it away?'

'Yes well, I was told that you were... the best. And professional,' Mr. Boyle said as he pointedly looked down his nose.

'Always am,' Shaw had agreed. 'Pride myself in it. I got word that you've got some money burning a hole in your pocket, and you want to spend it on getting something in those woods of yours removed.'

'I've been meaning to do something about it for a while now.' Mr. Boyle gestured vaguely towards the fuzzy outline of expansive woods past an open field behind the mansion. He kept his words very guarded. 'Of course, it's not wandered onto the main grounds, but it's only a matter of time until it does, and I can't

have anything like *that* out there cause any sort of...
bad press. It's a liability.'

'And just what exactly is *that* out there?' Shaw had
pointed at the woods. 'Bear or somethin'?'

'No. it's not a bear.' Mr. Boyle spoke slowly, not
meeting Shaw's eyes. 'I'll be honest with you, Mr.
Shaw, I don't know what it is.'

'You ever go out in those woods?' Shaw picked at
his tooth with a dirty, chipped fingernail.

'Oh heavens no, I've got no business with it.'

'Don't hunt?' Shaw hadn't bothered to hide his
contempt.

'That sort of thing doesn't attract me. I don't even
own a gun, but I'm more than willing to rent the woods
out to colleagues who do.'

'What's stopping you from letting them pay you to
hunt it then?' Shaw realized as he looked back on the
conversation, that he should have been more
suspicious. He'd been too eager, the prospect of money
clouding his judgement. Not like it would have
mattered. He'd have taken the job, suspicious or not.

'I have my reasons.' Mr. Boyle retorted. 'Are you up
for the task or not, Mr. Shaw?'

Shaw had laughed at that. 'Now, how could I turn

down ten thousand dollars and the opportunity to hunt on such fine, exclusive property?' he sneered at Mr. Boyle. 'Let me guess, that money ain't just for the animal is it? You want me to keep my mouth shut, is that right?'

Mr. Boyle had glared at him. 'If you're willing, I'll have you sign the paperwork. I want it dead, but bring it back in one piece.'

Shaw had taken that as a very clear "yes".

Even now, as he looked back on it, pulling his wrung-out clothes back on, he wasn't sure what the secrecy was about. Sure, they were weird looking animals, but what didn't Joseph Boyle want his rich buddies to know? Why not take the opportunity to make a profit off of exclusive game?

But Mr. Boyle's strange decision meant money in Shaw's pocket, so he wouldn't question it. Whether he was dealing with aliens from outer space or a science experiment gone wrong, his only job was to pump it full of lead and dump it on Mr. Boyle's immaculate back porch.

Though not as dry and prepared as he would have liked, Shaw hitched his reassembled shotgun over his shoulder and began the trek upstream. It was thanks to the river running a straight course that he knew he wasn't lost, but how far he was from his truck he couldn't say. It was going to get dark in an hour or two and he didn't fancy getting caught out alone and unprotected.

He made his way cautiously, alert, darting glances to the treetops and underbrush at the faintest sound. He was hyper aware that his boots still sloshed from the wet, his socks still soggy and gross on his bare skin. The bird song and murmuring of the river did nothing to relax him.

The cabin, nestled in a clearing with a view of the river, was a welcome surprise. But it made sense that it was there, and Shaw was more than relieved to see it. After all, Boyle had mentioned renting the woods to his buddies, so of course they'd be accommodated by a comfortable hunting lodge. At the very least it gave Shaw a new option to consider, and it was a favorable one. On one hand, he could stay the night mostly secure from whatever might be lurking in the dark, waiting for him, and on the other there might be some supplies he could use, like ammo.

He approached the back door, boots creaking against the wooden steps, still making sure to glance around, listening for suspicious noises. He pressed his face against the window, but it was too dark to get a good look. He doubted anyone was currently staying inside, not if Boyle was dealing with a "liability" as he put it.

Shaw gritted his teeth. He'd been expecting to sleep in his truck if the hunt took days, and knowing that this luxury hadn't been mentioned was an insult.

He tried the door, but as to be expected it was locked. Shaw went down the steps and tried the front door, but that was locked too.

He was more than happy to break down the door, if only to vent his frustration, but it didn't come to that. On second glance, he saw that one of the front windows was open, raised just high enough to get his hands under. It lifted with a groan of wood and Shaw swung one long leg inside, ducking his head as pulled the rest of his body after it.

The floorboards creaked as he meandered along, taking in his surroundings with a few nods of approval.

'Not bad,' he whistled. 'Not bad at all.'

It was nothing elaborate, only one floor, with an open layout and a high angled ceiling. Everything from the double bed, the kitchen, and the dining table was in the same space, no doubt a rich man's idea of "roughing it". The few doors he found to open only lead to a bathroom with a standing shower and a few closets. It was cozy, and stylishly furnished. It even had a chandelier, and the bed was made with a heavy white comforter and several lacey throw pillows.

Shaw began to search the place, opening drawers and cupboards as he stomped about on the hunt for canned food. Now he had a moment to relax, he realised that he was ravenously hungry, today's excitement having worked up his appetite. Wrenching open one of the cabinets revealed a few cans of clam chowder probably left by the last guests. Even better, the cans had pull tops. Shaw tore open the can, and snatched a spoon from the dish drainer, wolfing down the cold, gloppy chunks of concentrated soup without bothering to get a bowl or heat it over the stove. Fishy-smelling chunks caught on his chin and he wiped them back into his mouth with the palm of his hand.

He slowed down, scraping his spoon around the inside of the can. A bit odd, that there were dishes in the drainer, and not the drawer. Not unheard of, but if a past guest had forgotten to put them away, why wasn't there a layer of dust?

And why were there dirty dishes still in the sink, and trash in the trash can? All of which seemed fresh – and there was no mould, or rotten odour. There was a film of dried and greasy soap bubbles around the rim of the sink drain too, as if someone had pulled the plug not too long ago.

Shaw licked his spoon, contemplating what this could mean in his head, when he heard a soft noise. It reminded him of a cat.

A stray cat wandering into the woods was possible. Shaw clucked his tongue, placing the empty soup can on the counter, calling softly.

'Here, kitty kitty.' He fidgeted with the hilt of his hunting knife. An animal was just meat and skin after all, and meat was meat.

Another soft mewl, and now he knew it was inside the house. Somewhere by the bed if he had to guess. He approached slowly, clucking his tongue again.

He heard a clear response again. He'd overlooked that the bottom drawer of the bedside table was open a crack. From inside it, something mewled.

Cautiously, Shaw pulled it open all the way and almost dropped his hunting knife. 'The hell –'

Staring up at him, surrounded in a nest of sheets,

was a baby.

A human baby.

It blinked up at him, squinting against the bright light with a soft noise of complaint, fat little fists waving in protest at being interrupted from a nap. Looking hardly old enough to crawl or even sit up, the baby was clean, plump and healthy, dressed in a yellow onesie with bumblebees embroidered on the chest. It blinked up at him with very little interest, before yawning and sticking a pudgy hand into its drooling mouth, tufts of blond hair swirling about in unkempt little wisps.

Shaw's mouth hung open, his eyes bulging.

At least the answer to this mystery was a simple one.

Squatters. That would account for the dishes, the trash, and the food.

But where was the mother now? The baby was washed, well fed, and aside from being hidden in a dresser and left on its own, it looked cared for.

'Whatever,' he grunted, twirling the hunting knife in his fingers to thrust it back into the holster. 'Ain't my problem.'

He didn't have any use for babies, and this one was

an unwelcome inconvenience that he'd have to keep quiet if he wanted to stay the night.

There was a thud outside the cabin, like a large branch falling close to the porch. Shaw's hand instinctively tensed over his knife; slinking low towards the window, he peered out.

He couldn't see anything, but he heard the creak of floorboards to his right. The hairs on the back of his neck prickled.

He probed his tongue against his still-throbbing gums and licked his dry lips. From behind him the baby let loose a loud squeal.

Outside, there was a shuddering gasp, like a sob.

Relieved, Shaw poked his head out the window. 'Come on out, I've got your kid in here,' he snapped. 'And I don't have all –'

He gazed into a pair of huge, saucer eyes bulging in a round, furry face. It crouched low against the porch, forelegs bent like a spider, bat-like ears flattening as it let out a furious hiss full of razor-sharp teeth.

Shaw scrambled back with a strangled yell, hitting his head against the window frame in his haste. The beast followed after him, already halfway through the window, long-taloned fingers scraping against wood as it forced its way inside, snarling and shrieking at him.

'The hell you will!' Shaw roared, kicking the dining table with his full strength, laughing wildly as the monster screamed on impact.

With a swipe from both front legs, the beast sent the table toppling over with a crash. It slunk inside the cabin, crouched and hissing.

They circled each other, Shaw gripping his knife and making no sudden movements.

Confused and distressed, the baby was screaming its tiny lungs out.

The beast darted to the side suddenly, scuttling like a crab not towards Shaw, as he'd expected, but towards the makeshift crib, claws outstretched.

He didn't know what made him do it. Selflessness wasn't in his nature, and it wasn't as if he cared one way or another what happened to the brat. He should have let the beast be distracted by easy prey and made his getaway out the door.

But he didn't.

He lunged, sprinting and catching the beast by the neck in a football style tackle, burying his knife into one of its huge hands. It screamed, rocking its shoulders and reaching with a free hand to shake him off. Blood splattered against the wood floors and pure white bedsheets. Shaw dropped back, scooping up the baby and tucking it firmly against his chest as he dashed across the cabin and vaulted out the window, almost rolling across the porch. Adrenaline kept him going, thundering down the path and into the woods without looking back, the monster's screams and the baby's frightened wails echoing through the trees and inside his head.

Stinging from the humiliation of a retreat, he paused long enough to bellow at the cabin for the sake of his pride. 'This ain't over between us! I'm just getting started!'

He would end things alright; just as soon as he had a dry shotgun and fresh ammo, he'd be on top and the hunt would be on.

Shaw was regretting his moment of altruism. His swollen jaw throbbed mercilessly, his damp clothes were chafing him raw, and worst of all, the brat wouldn't stop crying. Its ear-splitting wails seemed to pierce right through Shaw's head and into his sore gums. They echoed into the woods, ringing among the trees so everything within earshot was aware of his location. His clumsy, inexperienced efforts to soothe the stupid thing only caused it to wriggle and writhe in his arms, fussing and drooling.

He had also realized that he couldn't aim a shotgun and hold a baby at the same time.

When it let out an excruciatingly piercing shriek, Shaw finally snapped. Holding it out in front of him, he gripped it under the armpits and snarled.

'Shut up! If you make another noise I'm gonna bash you against a tree before you get us both killed!'

The baby stared at him with wide eyes, before its plump face collapsed into a whimper, starting up a mewling, anxious cry.

Shaw groaned, cradling it with one arm and pinching the bridge of his nose as he fought his blood pressure. He took deep, steadying breaths.

This was a temporary setback. He just had to get to his truck and then the kid could be someone else's responsibility. He'd found it on Joseph Boyle's property, and that made it Boyle's problem.

He had a pretty good idea what had happened to the mother. He'd not found any evidence of it, but most likely she'd become lunch for a certain bat-eared freak.

'You're stuck with me,' he hissed down at the softly whimpering infant. 'Mommy isn't here and I ain't your Daddy. I ain't changing you, or feeding you, so the sooner we're out of each other's lives, the happier we'll be, got it?' He prodded it in its chubby stomach. 'So. Keep. Quiet. I got the gun, and I got the knives, so I make the rules around here.'

It whined piteously. Shaw hadn't bothered to check if it was a boy or a girl, and he didn't care. All it really boiled down to was a pain in his ass.

'You've got some nerve complaining. Could act a little grateful. If I weren't such a sweet, kind-hearted man I'd have left you,' he grumbled, more to himself. He knew perfectly well it couldn't understand a word he was saying, but it probably sensed his tone. 'Think that big furry bitch would have played nice with you? She'd have split you open and pulled out your insides, inch by inch.' Then he growled as an afterthought. 'And the next time we see her, I'll gut her myself so she can spend the rest of her days mounted to a wall.'

He continued his trek at a steady clip, keeping close to the riverbank. He was confident that he'd bought himself some time by pinning his pursuer to the floor, but it was only a matter of time till she got loose again. The sound of the river masked his footsteps but that also meant it would be difficult for him to hear her coming, so he paused intermittently to listen for anything other than the typical woodland noises.

The trees stretched out before him endlessly, the dim light of evening muffled by the shadow of the woods, and it was only the steady upward incline of the bank that let him know he was nearing his destination.

'See that?' he pointed, breathing heavily. 'That's where I shot the first one. We're close now.' He increased his speed, boots slipping against the dirt. 'With any luck there'll be something left of it when we get there,' he grinned, slipping again and catching himself on a branch. 'And once I take out our batty friend back there, that'll be twenty thousand dollars for me. And if Boyle thinks of paying me any less, I'll gut him too!'

It was the thought of such a huge payout in his future that gave him new energy.

The baby's eyes were closed, exhausted from all the excitement and tears. Its chubby little hands were tucked under its chin, nestled into a tight ball against Shaw's heaving chest.

'Kinda cute for dead weight. When you keep your mouth shut,' Shaw sneered.

But when he crested the hill and caught sight of his truck his improved mood vanished.

The bed was empty.

Completely empty; not so much as a scrap was left as evidence to show anything had ever been there. Shaw squatted and examined the bungee cords that had fallen to the dirt. He'd fit them securely, there was no way an animal could have unravelled them.

He swore, kicking one of the tires and flinging his shotgun into the dirt. He placed the fully awake and snivelling infant onto the hard surface of the ribbed truck bed so that he could pace, stamping and kicking, cussing a blue streak and ranting at the injustice of it all.

'Are you telling me she untied the body and ate the entire thing?!' he roared, waving his hands in the air. 'That ain't possible! I'll tell you one thing.' he pointed at the baby, who was watching him with big, scared eyes. 'I ain't about to be thrown off a cliff, half drowned, forced to babysit, and have my merchandise robbed from me just so I can go back to Boyle empty-handed with my tail between my legs! I'm getting that ten thousand dollars and I'm keeping my pride, y'hear?! And SHUT UP!'

The brat had started to whine again, snot and drool dribbling down its red, wrinkled face. Shaw was glad he'd never had any kids – or a wife for that matter.

But he had to calm down. He had to be on his game, alert. Couldn't fly off the handle when he had a job to do.

And one way or another, he was going to do it. And to do that, he needed fresh, dry ammo.

He trailed a hand tenderly along the metal surface of his truck as he approached the driver's side door. It had suffered its share of dings and scrapes over the years, but each fresh score he could feel in the paint that was the result of a beast's claws, was another pinch of salt in his wounded pride.

With a snarl, he pulled the door handle, only for it to hold fast with a clunk. He made a couple more bad-tempered attempts, without any success. It was locked, but he couldn't remember locking it. He never had any reason to when he went hunting alone, away from civilisation, so it wasn't something he bothered with.

Growling to himself he jammed his hands in his pockets, searching for his keys. His rummaging grew more frantic, stamping and swearing with frustration as he realized that he didn't have them, until he was almost crawling on his hands and knees in the dirt in case he'd dropped them close by. The worst-case scenario was that he'd lost them in the woods or in the river. He stood up straight, kicking his front tire in disgust. On the other side of the truck something toppled over with a hollow, metallic noise.

Shaw went to inspect it.

So he was in luck after all. In all the excitement he'd forgotten he'd left his ammo box on the ground at the passenger side. He flung open the lid and began selecting new shotgun shells with rhapsodic pleasure.

Shaw stroked his loaded gun lovingly as the emasculating feelings of vulnerability melted away to be replaced by a predatory sense of power.

But he wasn't ready yet.

He knew the second he entered those woods he would be in her domain. She could come from above his head as well as the ground, and being injured would only heighten her spite and ferocity. Shaw

112

massaged his swollen gums as he thought this over.

His truck was locked, and though he could simply walk to Boyle's and ask for a locksmith, it was still a problem. Without being able to hide inside if things got nasty, he was left out in the open and vulnerable.

He needed to have control again, to take the hunt on his terms instead of waiting with no plan of action or decent vantage point.

Obviously, he needed a trap. She'd ambushed him, so it was only fair that he returned the favour.

He knew exactly where and how he could do it... but he needed bait.

Live bait.

He leaned against the bed of his truck, picking at his front teeth with his cracked fingernails, deep in thought. Something big and easy enough to be tempting; that would catch attention by scent or noise.

He glanced distractedly over his shoulder, still fondling his gun with his long, scarred fingers. The baby had calmed again once the shouting and stamping had stopped, and was curled up in a little ball, half asleep and sucking on a fat little fist.

Shaw grinned, a wide, crooked sneer full of jagged,

yellow teeth as an epiphany clicked the last piece of the puzzle into place.

Hidden under a canopy of leaves, his scent disguised by wet earth and loam as well as a few drops of deer urine for good measure, Shaw congratulated himself on his brilliance.

It wasn't like the kid would be missed by anyone; in fact no one but him knew it even existed. Besides, Shaw was confident he could take his shot before any sort of disfiguring or fatal mauling took place, so he'd come out of it looking like a hero. And if he couldn't fire in time, or it got caught in the crossfire, the body wouldn't be found – and if it did, it was all the beast's fault, and nobody would know the difference.

He'd situated himself in a clearing not far from his truck where a large stump of a fallen tree served as a landmark.

As well as a serving table.

He had to say, the kid had behaved beautifully, asleep for most of the prep work so that there was no worry about any beast activity off schedule. He'd tethered them to the trunk by the ankle with a wire cord he kept in his ammo box, just in case the brat got restless and tried to wriggle off. It seemed too young and small to get very far very fast, but he had to prepare for the worst.

Now, all he had to do was wait. It was only a matter of time before the bait got cold, hungry, or wet, and its anxious, ear piercing cries would fill the woods, broadcasting its location.

Shaw licked his lips in anticipation. Remaining still and waiting in silence was part of the job description, he was used to it, but his dark, hairy arms were riddled with goosebumps, his jaw set. The woods had grown dark, night having fallen into a peaceful sort of gloom, the trees full with the eerie sounds of melancholy. Their branches knit together into a threadbare canopy, the moon and stars caught and held there as if in the spools of a dreamcatcher's net. The babble from the river was a distant mumble, outdone by the serenade of crickets, wailing of cicadas, and the occasional call of a screech owl.

An ant crawled across Shaw's lip and he licked it away, crunching it between his teeth. He blinked away fragments of leaves from his eyes, not daring to lift his head to scan the treetops as much as he wanted to.

The peaceful night drew on, undisturbed.

Then in the distance, came a mournful, inhuman wail. Shaw's blood froze, splintering in his veins like shards of crystal. He clenched his teeth even harder, despite the pain in his right jaw. Around him, the nighttime noises ceased with all the abruptness of turning off a car radio.

On the trunk, a tiny body wriggled with a soft rustle of fabric and loose bark. It mewled, a confused, pitiful sound of distress. Shaw's heartbeat quickened, knowing what was coming.

In the woods ahead of him came another blood-curdling shriek.

As he knew it would, the baby gave an answering scream, a plaintive, desperate noise that pierced the night's silence. It took up its howling cries in succession, splitting the peace and breaking through the woods in a crescendo of answering echoes and hiccupping sobs.

From somewhere down the slope, branches cracked and leaves rustled, a heavy body approaching with gathering speed, its claws scraping rock and roots in its haste to investigate. A shriek rose with a thunderous growl.

The baby continued to sob, tiny pink fists flailing, legs kicking against the cord that kept it tied.

Shaw gripped his shotgun, finger hovering over the trigger as he held his breath. He licked his dry lips, his heart hammering with the exhilaration of a hunt.

A pair of huge saucer eyes gleamed unblinkingly from the darkness, fixated intently on the stump, framed between shrubs and tree trunks. The creature breathed raggedly from its upward sprint. It stepped forward, crouched and slinking like a cat, sniffing, ducking its head to avoid low hanging branches and thorns as it crawled on its belly, a limp in its right foreleg.

The baby continued to scream its lungs out.

The urge to pull the trigger was infuriating, hot beads of sweat dripping down Shaw's neck and back, soaking his flannel shirt and staining his pits, each howl from the tree stump piercing his nerves like needles.

Victory was so close. She was in range, but if he missed he lost the element of surprise and it was all over. She needed to be fully distracted. Ears like hers could hear the click of the trigger, despite the loud wails of an unhappy baby, and she was fast. He couldn't be hasty even though he was seething with the desire to blow her head from her shoulders.

As if his animosity could be sensed, the creature lifted its head, ears pricking. Shaw's heart and stomach turned to lead as those ginormous eyes met his.

Did it see him? If not, could it hear his heart beating against his chest, or the sound of his breathing?

Slowly, it backed away into the gloom until nothing was visible but moonlight glinting from two rounded orbs. Then in a rapid rustle of leaves, she dashed to the side and vanished.

Shaw didn't dare move a muscle, his shoulders tensing so hard his whole spine burned. Sweat and dirt stung his eyes. Where had she gone? Was she stalking behind him, preparing to pounce, or had she just decided to leave, recognizing the danger she was in on instinct? The baby's cries drowned out any telling noises he would normally be able to catch.

Shaw swallowed, his throat dry and sandy.

A twig fell, landing onto the ground an inch from his nose. Shaw's breath barely had a second to catch when it was completely stolen from him as a heavy weight slammed into his back, piercing, agonizing pain stabbing deep into his flesh and tearing, a resounding screech of animal ferocity deafening him.

Talons tore through his down vest, and flannel, ripping his back into ribbons. Shaw's gun fell from his grasp, his fingers slippery from sweat and fresh, hot blood. Rows of razor-sharp teeth buried themselves into his right shoulder. The beast shook him violently like a terrier with a rat, before sending him flying with a toss of its head. He skidded in the dirt and leaves, his back slamming against the trunk of a tree so hard he felt his shoulder blades crunch.

He lay there, stunned, bleeding out from a deep, jagged rip in his neck. He tried to stand, but his legs only jerked and wiggled uselessly. His throat and mouth filled with hot blood which trickled from his mouth and nose. He opened his mouth and only managed a gurgle.

He watched, vision fading as the beast approached the stump, the baby's screams, previously loud and distracting, buzzing only faintly in his ears the way a radio signal is lost through a tunnel.

Licking Shaw's blood from its muzzle, the bat-like thing loomed over the stump and lowered its round, nearly snoutless head close. The baby's crying softened into breathless hiccups, distracted. Two chubby hands reached, tangling into the thick brown fur. Shaw waited for it to be snapped up, pulled apart and chewed.

The beast rubbed his face against the baby's fleece onesie with a low contented hum, the way a cat might mark its scent. Then it sat back, and raised both of its huge, uncannily human-like hands, one swollen and bloody, and hooked its jaws with its fingers, wrenching its mouth the same way you'd force open a rusty box. Like the seams of fabric, thick fur tore and ripped, mouth opening wider and wider until it peeled away entirely, and collapsed onto the forest floor in a heap like a loose and unzipped garment.

A woman stepped out, pale and naked, soft brown hair draped over her curved, ample breasts and curtaining her face from view.

She fell to her knees beside the stump, tugging the wire cord loose from the baby's ankle, and scooping it up, clutching it desperately to her chest. She buried her face into its wispy blond hair, rocking back and forth, her shoulders heaving as her entire body trembled.

Shaw watched this through fading vision, losing

even the ability to feel shocked, as each breath of air was a battle.

She stood, bending down and gathering up her cast-off fur coat, draping it over her shoulder like a toga, tenderly swaddling her baby with the loose ends. Long, grotesque arms like empty gloves dragged on the forest floor, the limp leather flaps of huge, bat-like ears hung across her shoulder. She bent her head and whispered something inaudible against her baby's ear before kissing the top of its fuzzy head, soothing it into uneasy silence. The infant still gurgled and whimpered, but safe in the arms of its mother, it began to relax.

She then turned and glared at Shaw, eyes far less huge, but still gleaming with pure hatred, a look of loathing that he returned with all the energy he could muster.

With the last of his strength, Shaw gurgled out a final parting word as she walked past him.

'Bitch.'

She paused, scowling down at him. Then her hateful expression softened into a playful smile and she held out her hand, one finger crooked.

Shaw's keys dangled above his head, jingling softly

as glints of moonlight reflected off of their jagged surface before she snapped her hand closed and turned her back on him, picking up his fallen shotgun with her free hand and disappearing up the slope.

He heard the sound of an engine starting in the distance as his vision grew dark, the forest floor hungrily soaking up his lifeblood like an offering.

POWER LINES

by Michael R. Goodwin

Strong wind whipped snow and ice against the windows, tapping an erratic staccato on the old glass. Drifts of snow snuck their way in through cracks around the door. The small hunting cabin I happened upon in the woods was built by no master carpenter, but it was shelter in a storm when I had none and for that I was grateful.

I had gone down back for a walk on my property when the storm hit. Sudden squalls and snow showers aren't unheard of in Maine, especially in February. In the valley where my property lies, the weather as predicted by the local news doesn't always apply. Before this excursion I had the foresight to put on my heavy parka and thick gloves. I had been caught unprepared once or twice before, which were lessons hard learned.

The reason for the walk was simple: I had heard the

sound of heavy machinery coming up from the woods, and I intended to investigate.

Some time ago, Central Maine Power had purchased a section of my land so that they could run high voltage lines between the substations in Vassalboro and the new one they built behind the fairgrounds here in Webster Mills. I wasn't keen on the idea, but I could either sell the parcel of land or have it forcibly taken from me. There was no sense arguing with a company as big as CMP so I opted to take the cash, which made dealing with their intrusion slightly more bearable.

The sound of machinery was likely coming from those power lines. Had this been a clear summer day, I wouldn't have thought twice about it. CMP was often down there, making repairs and cutting down brush. But it was the middle of winter and we'd had close to three feet of total snowfall so far this season. The sound was much louder than the Anderson kids ripping through on their snowmobiles, so I figured I owed it to my peace of mind to check it out.

I grabbed my .30-30 rifle from my gun cabinet before I left for some additional peace of mind. The words of my father echoed in my head as I threw a handful of brass rounds into the pocket of my parka.

Better to have and not need, than to need and not have.

It took me about twenty minutes to make it from my house to the power lines. As the crow flies it was probably a quarter mile or so, but the trail I followed added a little extra distance with its curves and turns. Walking through the deep snow slowed me down a little, but I was in no rush and didn't need to break a sweat getting there. I had slung my rifle on my back and reminded myself to keep an eye on the time. Dusk arrived around 17:00, full dark around 18:00, but I knew I'd be back home long before then.

At least I thought I would.

I followed the sound of machinery through the woods. Clattering and clanging and grinding, blasts of pneumatic pumps, peppered with heavy thumps that shook the ground. The noise got louder as I approached, but the closer I got, the more... *menacing* the sounds became. They sounded impatient and violent, like someone swinging a sledgehammer against the steel doors of a crypt, shaking the chains bound around the door handles, trying to free the dead who were locked inside.

I tried to push aside those thoughts before they got away from me. I've always had a bit of an imagination, but the sounds I followed weren't the product of that.

They were real, and just ahead.

An overgrowth of grass and brush obscured the view of the wide incision CMP had made through the trees. I reached the field just before 13:00, expecting to see the collection of large construction vehicles and other equipment that had been assaulting my ears for the last few hours.

Instead, I saw... nothing.

The expanse of field was empty, except for the high voltage towers that loomed above like headless giants standing guard, connected to each other by thick cables.

The field was empty, yet the sound of the machinery was louder than ever.

The noise was deafening, and I felt like I was in the middle of one of the invisible machines itself. I could feel the heat of the exhaust buffeting against my face, and could smell the pungent sweet odor of engine oil. The ground underneath me and the air around me trembled, and I became scared.

The noise was here, but where was the noise *coming* from?

I placed my gloved hands over my ears and wandered further into the swath of open land. Standing underneath one of the headless giants, I turned a slow circle to see if there was anything further up or down the field. From my vantage point on the ground, there was nothing and nobody out here except me.

Something didn't feel right, and hadn't felt right since I stepped into the field. The only thing I knew was that my eardrums couldn't take much more of the noise, so I headed back towards the trail, trying to convince myself of an explanation my frenzied imagination had cooked up.

It was simple, see? The noise was carried down into the valley from some nearby logging operation. It would explain everything... except it didn't explain the blasts of hot exhaust I felt on my face, or that distinct smell of oil and hot metal. There was no easy explanation for that. Ignoring that thought like the vision of the crypt door, I focused on the task at hand, which was getting the hell back on the trail towards home.

It was then that I saw the storm.

To my left up on the Webster Mills side, a low cloud broiled on the horizon. Dark and churning, the cloud sunk down into the valley like ink in water. It startled me how dark the rest of the sky was, realizing then that dusk was upon me. I checked my watch, and saw that it was 16:45.

I had somehow lost almost four hours standing in this place, this place of invisible machines and unseen storerooms for the dead. Panic crawled its way up into my heart, despite my best efforts to remain calm. I had been caught with my ass in the wind before, and told myself this was no different.

Except I had never seen a storm move this fast in my life. The storm cloud rushed down like a runaway train towards where I stood, frozen in fear. I saw great gusts of wind and snow underneath the cloud, which hung low enough to make the high voltage towers evaporate under its veil.

The sound of the approaching storm rose up, eliminating the noise of the invisible machinery that had brought me down here to begin with. There was just the wind, the wind.

A blast of fine ice and snow hit me square in the face, and that got me moving.

I spun around, looking for the trail that had led me here. I spotted it and ran, just making it beyond the treeline when the storm passed overhead.

The trees surrounding me groaned and leaned to one side in unison under the force of the wind and snow. Even with the pines and birches breaking up the gust of wind, the force of it through the trees was still almost strong enough to knock me down. I braced myself and let instinct take over.

I had been walking on this trail since I was nine years old. There was no dip or angle of this path that I did not recognize, so all I had to do now, storm and snow and wind be damned, was simply trust my gut.

Snow was falling in heavy sheets. In the looming darkness, it made everything in front of me nearly impossible to see. I trudged forward, leaning into the wind.

The woods became full of furious noise. It was a symphony of chaos; the howling wind standing in for the chorus, strains of menacing machinery the low brass, and the snapping and cracking of tree limbs and branches the percussion.

Requiem for an Anxiety Attack, I thought to myself. It was then that I realized I had no clue at all where I was.

That was when I saw the cabin.

I knew, even through my delirium, that there was no such cabin on my land.

Yet there it stood, about a hundred feet ahead. I caught glimpses of it through gaps in the curtains of snow and ice, and headed straight for it.

Again, my brain tried to solve this mystery for me.

I must have gotten turned around and on the wrong trail, the one that led into the woods on the far side of the power lines. I was already scared, starting to panic, and must have turned left instead of right.

Except I knew that couldn't be the case, as I had seen my deer stand up in the trees, knocked upside down from the wind but exactly where I had hung it years before on the near side of the power lines.

I may not have been able to see where I was going very well, but I sure as hell hadn't turned completely around in the opposite direction.

Right?

No, I would have seen the high voltage towers standing watch in the field.

I decided it didn't matter where I was. I had an opportunity to get out of the storm, and I should take it. I staggered up to it, exhausted and legs shaking, freezing cold yet sweating under my parka in defiance of the frigid temperatures. I couldn't work the doorknob under my thick gloves, so I slipped one off. The freezing metal bit into my skin as I gripped and turned, and then the door opened outward.

The wind took the door and slammed it open against the wall of the cabin. Gusts of wind carried snow inside, so I stepped into the cabin and wrestled the door shut.

The cabin was small, no more than ten feet square. It had two windows, both facing the field where the power lines stood: one from the south, one from the east. I could see the headless giants in the field, gripping the high voltage cables that swung in the wind like murderous jump ropes.

In the fading light, I found a metal folding chair in one corner and a small wood stove in another. In the third corner was a stack of firewood, and in the fourth, a five-gallon bucket.

What more did a hunting cabin need? A place to sit, something to help keep you warm, and a bucket to piss in.

The cabin was cold, but warmer than it was outside. I set about making a fire in the stove, happy to find a box of matches resting on top of the woodpile. After arranging some wood inside the belly of the stove, I slid open the matchbox and picked out a match.

Wind sucked the door to the cabin open and caught a greedy finger on the match box, wanting to prize them away. I shoved the box into my pocket and scrambled to shut the door. Once I had it closed again, I spotted a broom handle leaning up against the studs to one side of the door. I slipped the handle through the metal door pull that served as the interior doorknob to hold the door closed.

The wind tried to sneak open the door again, but the improvised lock held strong.

Redneck ingenuity, I chuckled to myself.

The firewood in the cabin was dry and eager to burn. It took only minutes for the small stove to be roaring with flames, sharing not only blessed warmth but also light.

The flickering glow of the fire was the only light I had as full dark closed in outside. Malaise settled deep within me like heavy sediment as I hunkered down near the stove to warm up, bringing myself to accept the reality that this was where I would be spending the night.

Inside, the fire roared.

Outside, the wind howled.

Somewhere else, the sounds of machinery persisted.

They'd been at it a while, wherever they were.

I wondered how long it'd take for them to get that crypt door to open.

*

It didn't take long for the small space to warm up. Within an hour I had stripped off my parka, hanging it over the stove to dry out. My boots and socks were next, followed by my snow-soaked blue jeans.

My rifle was leaning muzzle-up in the corner behind me. I had taken the handful of cartridges out of my jacket pocket before hanging it above the stove and loaded them into the gun's magazine. I racked the lever to chamber a round, and then stuffed one more cartridge into the magazine. I wasn't about to spend a night in the woods any more unprepared than I already was.

I sat in my boxers on the floor, using the metal folding chair as a drying rack, feeling fortunate to have found this mystery cabin. Yet, as grateful as I felt to be out of the storm, I couldn't shake the feeling that I was somewhere I wasn't supposed to be.

This very cabin, for example.

It shouldn't exist, didn't exist, but here it was.

I would have noticed its construction, as it was on the edge of the trail I walked on at least once a week, regardless of the season. There was no way that it had been built since the last time I had been down this way, judging by the layer of dust on the woodstove and the cobwebs in the corners of the ceiling.

As much as I tried to explain it, I found I could not. The cabin either existed, or I was having one hell of a hallucination.

'This must be real,' I said aloud, though the inflection in my voice made it sound like I was questioning even myself.

Outside, the wind picked up speed. The cabin shook and the windows rattled in their frames. Icy drafts pushed their way into the cabin and the flames in the woodstove flared up with the fresh incentive to burn.

I got up and placed another log in the stove. The flames caught on quickly, fighting against the cold that intruded through the uninsulated walls. I checked my clothes and, finding them dry and warm, eagerly put them back on. I slipped on my parka and boots, even though I had no intention of leaving this cabin until daylight, even if I did feel like I was trespassing.

For now, I had everything that I truly needed.

Shelter from the freak nor'easter happening outside, a warm fire crackling in the woodstove beside me, and dry clothes.

I dragged the metal folding chair over to one side of the stove. I sat down, positioning myself with my back against the wall. My rifle was within arm's reach, loaded and ready to go should the need present itself.

The warmth in the cabin made my eyelids heavy.

Sleep came, swift and sudden, like the storm raging outside.

The sound of the machinery pervaded my dreams, preventing much sleep at all. I couldn't tell how long I had been asleep, as my watch had died sometime after my arrival at the cabin.

The sounds came from a fleet of grotesque contraptions with hungry blades. Under the light of the moon they dug deep trenches in the ground and revealed forgotten skeletons buried below. They wriggled free of the rocks and roots that had pinned them down and crawled up from the earth, gusts of snow swirling around them like wintry capes. Without any hesitation, each one joined in the effort.

Digging, unearthing.

Exhuming.

This skeleton crew – a name divined by the monarch of Bangor – toiled under the storm clouds. Trench after trench they dug, freeing scores of their brethren.

There were animals, too. The bones of countless deer, foxes, and coyotes mixed among the bones of men and women, lending a hoof or a paw to turn up the earth that had taken them all underneath its folds.

Together they dug, uprooting the headless giants holding the high voltage lines, causing them to tumble to the ground. Great showers of sparks exploded from the severed power lines, thick black snakes spewing their venom into the air.

I watched them dig from my trailside haven. The ground shook under the violence of their machinery, tearing up roots like tendons off flesh. The legion of skeletons of all species grew to an innumerable size, a field of bones transforming into an army above the earth, one body at a time.

And then the machinery suddenly powered down. The spinning blades and augers slowed to a stop, hydraulic arms with deep scoops paused in mid-dig. Those armed with shovels and pick-axes dropped their tools, joining those who climbed down from their perch on the rusted machines around a massive pit. The animals among them pawed at the ruined earth, restless.

The absence of noise and vibration from the machinery made everything feel empty and still. Snow still fell rapidly around them, applying a pure white carpet over the fresh turned earth.

It was impossible to see beyond the crowd of skeletons, to get a glimpse of what caused them to suddenly stop digging. They packed in tight, bones knocking against each other in a way that sounded like hollow rain.

Then all at once, the skeleton crew stood still.

A shockwave burst outward from the pit, rippling through the crowd and sending skeletons flying in pieces in every direction. It continued into the woods, knocking down trees and creating huge drifts of snow in its wake.

I thought for sure the cabin I was hiding in was going to be decimated, but somehow it held together against the shockwave. Hurricane winds pushed through the cracks in the walls, strong enough to knock me to my knees and snuff out the fire burning in the woodstove, plunging the cabin into darkness.

In the seconds it took my eyes to adjust to the dark, at least enough to discern the glow of the suffocating embers in the woodstove, I heard a new, different noise.

This noise was made available to my ears because the sound of the storm, I realized with a sickening dread, had diminished after the shockwave.

The noise was faint but advancing.

It was the sound of footsteps and hooves, crunching on icy snow.

Hundreds of them, possibly thousands.

I crawled to the window and peered out to see the army of skeletons walking up the trail. Adversaries in life, now comrades in death.

Terrified, I fell to the floor of the cabin and crawled over to my rifle. I doubted that it would do much good, but a dark voice in my mind assured me that I could always save one bullet for myself.

The footsteps in the snow grew louder and louder, until that was all I could hear. It sounded like eminent demise, the incessant *crunch, crunch, crunch* of dry bones against snow.

They surrounded the cabin, the noise of their fleshless feet like a blanket of panic that smothered the cabin, and gathered close. Close enough to each other for me to hear their bones clacking together, close enough to the cabin for me to feel the knocks of their bodies against the walls. Once they were tucked in tight, they stopped stamping their feet.

In the dark, surrounded by a legion of skeletons that had come from underneath an electric corridor, I gripped my rifle tight. The only noise, save for the beating of my own heart, was the strong wind whipping snow and ice against the windows, tapping an erratic staccato on the old glass.

Was it the wind?

Or was it one of my visitors, asking to come inside?

I took one hand off my rifle and felt for the woodpile. I found a piece of birch and threw it into the woodstove. The embers considered it, and then ate the birch bark eagerly, fire springing to life and spreading light once again.

Shadows danced, and I saw something pulling on the door.

The broom handle shifted in its place as the door rattled in its frame, shaken from the outside. The wooden bar bowed outward, cracking and splitting under the pressure.

It had held against the wind, but whatever was pulling on it now was much stronger.

I got to my feet and shouldered my rifle.

The broom handle shattered and the door flew open.

Outside, under the glow of the moon, were the skeletons. Human and animal standing together in their unlikely union. A massive buck stepped forward to the front of the crowd, the needle-sharp points of its massive rack gleaming in the moonlight.

I fired my rifle, the sound of gunfire painfully loud in the confined space. The shot struck the buck in the chest, knocking it and those nearby backwards like bowling pins. More rushed in behind them, pushing their way into the cabin.

They gnashed their teeth, and I knew what they wanted.

Somehow, I just knew.

I racked the lever of my rifle and fired again. Again. Again.

Four shots fired. How many did I have left?

Should I save one for me?

The skeletons pressed their way into the cabin. Some came in the proper way, through the door. Others broke through the old windows and pulled themselves in that way. Others pounded their bony hands or hooves or paws against the walls until the walls cracked and gave way.

I fired again, climbing onto the metal chair, though I knew there was no escape.

The muzzle of rifle was hot, the acrid smell of gunpowder making my nostrils flare. It burned the skin underneath my chin.

I had one round left, but when I squeezed the trigger, nothing happened.

There was no loud report from my gun. Just a click, signalling that the last round in the chamber was a dud and would not fire. I let it tumble to the floor, as it was now useless to me.

I felt something bump into me from behind.

The surge of skeletons paused.

I turned and saw a man hanging from a noose tied to the rafters. The sight of him did not frighten me, but how I had missed seeing the evidence of this suicide earlier, I do not know.

He had been there a while, little more than dried out tendons holding his bones together under his parka and jeans.

His parka, or mine? They looked identical.

He was hanging over the stove, which was now cold and full of grey ash.

I turned back and the cabin spun around me, sawing side to side.

My rifle, rusted and decrepit, lay at my feet.

The skeletons who had pushed their way in through the cabin door took me down from my noose and stripped me of my clothes so that I looked like them.

Bones, bare and white.

Together we walked out to the field and down into the pit.

At the bottom of the pit was the crypt. A sledgehammer propped open one of the massive steel doors.

So they finally got it open, I thought.

The other door opened, and the skeleton crew ushered me inside.

IN THE BEGINNING
by Carla Eliot

Knowledge is sweet. But it can also be deadly.

In an irreversible moment the scales fell from my eyes and I saw that all was *not* good – this marked the true beginning.

That other beginning that was forced upon me was *his* beginning – the man, the God, one and the same. His wants were my wants. His desires, my desires. There was no questioning any of this. Woman was made from man and was part of man, so belonged to man. The animals around us were a reflection of us, only slightly distorted. Although some solitary creatures slithered around on their bellies while other larger, fiercer beasts lurked in their packs, they all bore the same raw animalistic instincts: hunt, eat and breed. We were no different from them, yet the God by my side controlled it all and until that irreversible moment I never really saw any of it.

But one day, something started to stir inside of me. A wriggling and writhing in the pit of my stomach like a wild snake fighting for freedom from the confines of my weak, female body. And that snake had a voice, a whispering rasping voice; cracking from misuse, it was difficult to understand immediately what it was trying to tell me. I finally quieted my frightened heart beneath its cage, and I listened.

The voice came from deep, deep within and it echoed a feeling, a yearning, a seed of passion that had been planted inside of me yet had never been given room to grow. When I recognised this passion I panicked. I didn't know what to do with this new longing. I tried to stamp on the snake so that the unsettled writhing and hissing would stop.

The snake dodged my feet and through its steadfast squirming it grew stronger. It wouldn't let me forget about that seed which promised so much more. I imagined what it could become. What it could grow into. I saw the shade it could offer me from the scorching sun. I saw the shelter it could provide from the beating rain. I could imagine the taste of that freedom as I bit into the crunchy apple that would grow from my labour of love.

I must have been sleeping for a long time – living a

life with my eyes open but seeing nothing, just his dreams and his visions.

I finally see the truth. And I allow myself to dream.

I study and admire our garden. The trees that he planted are beautiful. The small creatures that dart between the bobbing flowers are vivacious. Brightly coloured birds that soar in the clear sky are inspiring – my own heart soars just watching them.

But my heart weeps now, too. The colour of the blood pouring from the gaping hare's stomach is vivid. The fox scrabbles with his front paws at its kill, blood dripping from its mouth in lurid drops.

The steadiness of the ocean under a full moon reflects the calmness I can often feel, whilst the crashing of the waves in a wild storm represents my fear. I've never felt fear before. I witnessed it for the first time in the eyes of the lifeless hare. Now, I am aware of the myriad of emotions inside of me.

They aren't all good.

I can see further than these boundaries. There is more in the distance, beyond our garden.

Fields of green and yellow and glinting rivers winding through the high mountains.

The garden is no longer enough for me. I now know that I'm just a prisoner here.

He senses the change in me. He can see that my eyes are open and that I have noticed his naked body. I am ashamed of my own bare flesh and wrap myself in leaves.

'You will die,' he threatens. 'You came from dust and you will return to dust.'

'I have knowledge now,' I say. 'I know what is good and what is evil.'

'It was better when you knew nothing,' he replies.

The next morning is cool. I try to stay sheltered from the roaring wind by hiding in the crowd of trees. The dark clouds hang heavily, pressing against the overhanging branches. I am caught in a cobweb of shadows. My heart beats frantically as I sense that I'm not alone – where there's a web there has to be a spider.

I hold my breath and the wind seems to do the same. There is an unnerving silence, thick and all around me, touching my skin. I crouch between a tree and a thorny shrub, clutching the leaves tighter to my breasts.

A branch snaps under a stealthy tread.

I can hear footsteps. He has followed me, I realise.

He seems to be always watching. It's as if he knows my thoughts and resents my desire for freedom.

I keep still, listening as he creeps closer. Then as if commanded by him the wind breaks its vow of silence and begins roaring once more, smothering everything else.

The tiny hairs lift on the back of my neck and I swallow down a scream.

I can feel the breath of God on my skin. A whoosh of air brushes my vulnerable flesh and I shiver.

I swivel and stumble backwards, scrambling away from his powerful presence.

The space by the tree is empty.

I flick my eyes, searching for him in the shadows. Darkness seems to bleed from the pores of every surface – it pools and spreads closer towards me. I pull my legs in and curl up into a tight ball.

I can't see him, but I'm sure that he is watching me; I can feel his eyes wandering over my body and burning into my soul.

I shut my eyes and I will him to disappear. I pray that he'll leave me alone.

This time, my prayers are answered.

*

Light fades to darkness and darkness turns into light.

I barely sleep; alert to every sound, dreading his touch. I want to be left alone and yet I am already the loneliest creature in the garden.

In the world.

Every other living thing seems to be a part of a greater picture. They appear content to follow their flock, herd or pack, and they are resolute in carrying out their designated tasks.

They communicate to each other in ways that are foreign to me. My own thoughts and feelings are repressed as I have no one to share them with. No one who will listen.

I am apparently his equal; I was created in God's likeness. Then why do I feel ashamed?

Why do I feel trapped?

I don't believe him. I don't trust him. I no longer have faith in him.

The sun is a high yellow ball in a sky the same blue as a magpie's egg. I go down into the valley and sit by a fast-flowing stream. I dip my hand into the cold water and watch it pass by my fingers, wondering where it is travelling to.

Standing, I spring onto one of the slick rocks that pop above the water. I go to step onto the next one but the slimy surface of the rock slips beneath me and I fall sideways into the water.

For a moment I think about just letting the freezing water carry me along and seeing where it takes me. Natural instincts kick in, however, and I swim and claw my way back out.

I flop down to the grass, gasping for air. Eventually my racing heart slows and my breathing becomes natural, again. I allow the sun to kiss my skin and dry the droplets of water that fleck my body.

Lying there, I am suddenly aware of the pain emanating from my shoulder. I lift a hand and I'm surprised to feel a sticky warm substance. I look down at my hand and stare at my crimson fingers. I must have cut myself when I fell, maybe on one of the rocks; blood is pouring from the gash on my shoulder.

I crawl back to the stream and splash water over the cut. The blood forms a thin river down my arm and drips from my fingertips. As I watch the bright drops disperse in the water I am reminded of the hare and its lifeless eyes, and I remember the blood that stained the fox's little sharp teeth.

Sweat begins to tickle my top lip as a tingling

sensation like a thousand fingers runs over my scalp.

The familiar writhing snake in my stomach is back. It wriggles upwards, and wraps itself around the new seed that is already growing in my mind.

By the time the stream is running clear, the blood from my wound washed away, the seed has been replaced by a tree, and its roots are firmly set.

I know how I can be rid of him.

The trees tremble around me as I crawl in their shadows. Their leaves rustle and whisper above me and they shimmer and shift in the moonlight like a school of fish.

I don't know where he is, but I can sense him. He is never too far away.

I am trying to hide from him so that I can think – I need to make a plan. I'm afraid that as soon as he sees me he will know my thoughts and he will notice something different in my eyes. I am worried about the power he has over me and how weak he makes me feel.

'Why are you hiding from me?' His voice booms from behind me and seems to shake the ground beneath my hands and knees.

I jump to my feet and press my back against the trunk of a tree. The drumming of my heart rattles my ribcage as I search the darkness.

'Why are you afraid?' His words tumble towards me and I see something stir in the shadows.

I step back from the sound, retreating from the pulsing and watching darkness.

'Don't ignore me. Come out so that I can see you.'

I turn and break into a run.

Twigs snap under my feet and branches claw at my arms and legs. There's crashing through the trees behind me as he follows, gaining on me with every step. I can feel his cool breath on my neck and it sends a trickle of sweat down my spine, hot as lava.

I dart a look over my shoulder just as the moon finds a break in the trees. His naked body shines almost silver in the milky light. The rippling muscles of his arms and pumping legs remind me of his strength as he charges close behind. I remember how my own naked body had looked before covering and wrapping it in leaves.

I think about the long, dark hair that billows out behind me as I run. I imagine what I must look like to him as he draws closer and closer. The only bit of flesh that isn't covered in hair or leaves is the skin of my arms and legs. Those uncovered parts must be all he can see in the thick shadows that surround us.

I take a deep shuddering breath, pushing my legs and arms as fast as I can as I try to widen the gap between us.

I grab onto the trunk of the first tree that my hand finds and swing myself around in the direction I was just running from. The momentum of the turn gives me more speed, pushing me forward. Out of the corner of my eye I see a flash of white as he continues running by me. In one fluid movement I leap behind the nearest tree and drop to my knees. I tuck in my arms and plant the side of my cheek against the cool earth, my hair falling over the rest of my face.

Sucking in a breath, I listen.

The footsteps slow before coming to a stop. There's a pause. A sharp intake of breath.

Then a rustling as he retraces his steps, his feet kicking up leaves. His footsteps draw nearer.

I can feel the air moving around me. The ground vibrates beneath my face as he steps closer.

I stay still; not breathing; eyes clamped shut. I try to hear him above the banging of my heart.

'Where are you?' He calls and it echoes just above my head. I bite my bottom lip and clench my fists to stop the tremble that's threatening to run through my body.

'You should have nothing to hide from me.'

Leaves whisper somewhere in the darkness and a branch cracks not too far away from my ear.

His padding footsteps circle me and for a moment I think that he is deliberately trying to scare me until I realise that the sound is growing quieter – that it's actually fading.

I open my eyes and stare into the heavy blackness, waiting for them to adjust. My heart is still pounding wildly, pummelling the ground beneath my chest. I release my breath in a soft sigh. The whoosh of air lifts my hair slightly and I catch sight of something, just a short distance away from me, before my hair drops down, obscuring my vision once more.

His footsteps are faint; I can hardly hear him now.

I slip out an arm from under my chest and carefully creep my fingers across the forest floor. I search blindly for what I'd seen, but it doesn't take me long to find the hard, round object. I wrap my fingers around the cool surface of the rock and pull it towards me.

It wouldn't require a lot of force, I don't think. I'd probably only have to hit him with it once. Then I wouldn't need to worry about him anymore. I'd be alone. I'd be free.

'Where are you? You can't hide forever.'

I lift my head – searching the darkness – before crawling quickly to the nearest tree. I peer around the trunk towards his fading footsteps. Keeping my back against the tree, hand clutching the rock so tightly it feels like my hand might break, I push myself up to a standing position.

The squirming snake in my stomach lifts its head and nudges my heart. I'm about to take a step out from behind the tree, when I pause.

I suddenly picture what my days would be like without him. Long, empty days without his rules or the constant fear of being watched and followed.

My body would be my own. My spirit would be free. But what about my soul? How could I truly live a happy and peaceful life after doing what I'm about to do?

My black soul would burn and smoulder inside of me until there'd be nothing left but ash. I'd be a shadow of what I am now. That wouldn't be freedom; it would be hell. Although his physical body would no longer exist, God would still punish me.

I let the rock fall and I hear the heavy thud as it hits the ground.

My whole body is shaking. I'm not sure if it's from

fear, adrenaline or something else.

I come out from my hiding place and start to walk in the direction that I had heard him go. Eyes fixed on the darkness ahead I breathe the night in deeply – and then freeze.

I am not alone.

We are not alone. There is something else in the forest with us.

There's a flash of movement in the shadows just in front of me; a heaving form that is even blacker than the darkness it lurks in. It's gone before I can get a good look at it.

However, I had heard it breathing – a deep, pulsing snort. I had seen the cloud of steam pour from its nostrils.

I think of calling out to him, to warn him, but when I open my mouth the words stick in my throat.

A scream shatters the silence.

My heart flutters like a wild bird. I'm unable to move, fear locking me in place. All I can do is listen to his cries of pain as the sound bounces off the trees.

Wings flap frantically as birds shoot upwards towards the sky, out of the forest, and away from the awful noise.

His screams abruptly stop and the silence drops

heavily around me once more.

It takes me a long time to find the courage to move. I search the forest until a thin streak of amber in the sky marks another day.

I can't find him, and there's no sign of the thing that I'd glimpsed in the shadows.

I give up looking.

Some time passes.

I watch the sun rise countless times and I speak to the moon to quell my loneliness. My muscles grow weaker and my hands ache. When I glance at my reflection in the stream I can see that my hair has lost some of its colour; it changes to grey, to silver and then finally to white.

I am taking a walk through the forest when I hear a new sound.

I creep slowly towards the voices, keeping close to the shadows that I now know so well.

Hiding behind a large shrub, I push aside a few leaves to peer at the new creatures in the garden.

As I gaze at the man and woman a wave of raw emotion sweeps over me. They are both naked, just as I used to be. I haven't thought about those days for a long time, but looking at the vulnerable innocence of the woman before me I feel as if I could be gazing at my old self.

I watch them closely. How they interact with one another. How she listens to his every word and obeys his commands without questioning.

I know what I have to do, so I wait.

The light is fading when the man disappears further into the trees, leaving the woman alone.

I crawl out from my hiding place, still keeping to the shadows. I move softly along the ground, snaking my way around the trees. When I am close enough that I can almost touch her I stop, and go still. I don't want to scare her; I want her to trust me.

'Do you think you are free?' I whisper.

The woman turns her head, searching for me in the darkness. I come around the tree so that she can see me, but I stay low to the ground.

'You need to listen to the voice inside of you, so that you can know the truth.'

'What is the truth?' the woman asks.

'Let the seed inside of you grow. Allow the scales to fall from your eyes. Then you will see. Then you will know that all is not good.'

THE PERIGEAN TURN

by K.A. Schultz

Jonah-Blue was born blue, and Jonah-Blue was also more often blue than he was not – at least, that's the way Oma Thiele put it. I was regular and pink, and our Mama said I cried right on cue. Jonah-Blue, on the other hand, had all his insides squooshed up, way up inside of him when he was born, which was just a few minutes after I was born, so he didn't cry or fuss or hardly even move. Mama said they rushed him to the NICU, where they operated on him and moved all his insides back to their rightful places. Then they stitched up his chest. My little-by-a-few-minutes brother eventually turned a decent enough shade of pink that the doctors and nurses of the NICU let him go home. We were both about one month old by then.

If being born blue wasn't bad enough, Jonah-Blue spent most of his years with me feeling sort of blue, too. I wore lots of pink, as I usually felt bright and pastel-coloured feelings. I guess you could say I was as bright on the inside as I was on the outside. Oma Thiele called my little brother a melancholy sort of bean. That's what cinched his name for me. Blue from day one and Blue 'til day last. My little brother didn't even seem to mind the name I gave him; before too long, everyone was calling him that.

I still wonder if that was the right thing to do.

My bright-coloured feelings gave me lots of energy that last spring. I couldn't wait to get up and out of bed each morning. Mama would tell me she wished if only for once I would sleep in like all the other kids. I think she just wanted to sip her coffee and not have to say anything to anyone until her first cup was all gone. I also think she wanted to pretend she was a lady of leisure and not the single two-job working-mom she really was. My getting up so early got in the way of her daydream. I love my mother, so I at least had enough sense to stay quiet and fix my own breakfast. For about two years, though, all I ever had was Lucky Charms and milk. Jonah-Blue, on the other hand, would sleep all morning and lay awake all night in his bedroom, staring at the ceiling, his inside-clock all messed up, too. Oma Thiele also said Jonah-Blue was a nocturnal bean. Both Jonah-Blue and I liked the way Oma Thiele used such big words on us, even when I didn't always understand what she meant. I could at least feel what it was she was talking about. As we were sort-of-twins, Jonah-Blue and I didn't have to use many words at all. I usually knew what he was thinking, and Jonah-Blue understood me.

My bright-coloured feelings pulled me outdoors from morning 'til night. I had a pre-curfew, you could say; I was not allowed to strap on my metal roller skates and make up skate dances until our neighbours pulled out of their driveway in the morning for work. You can bet, just as soon as their cars pulled out, those metal skates were strapped on over my tennis shoes and away I would go. I pretended I was an Olympic skater competing for gold medals. Jonah-Blue would sometimes do the medal ceremony with me. We would sing our version of the National Anthem and I would fake cry. I'd even try to squeeze out real tears. Jonah-Blue would get bored with me, though, real quick, especially if I asked him to watch and clap for me when my skate dances were done. He'd just roll his big, blue eyes. By the way, my eyes were brown, which I hated. I wished my eyes could have been the colour of his – they were the colour of sea glass.

What Jonah-Blue liked best was to sit on the back

porch and read or draw.

Jonah-Blue's blue feelings gave him different kinds of energy. Oma Thiele called it Storm and Dung, whatever that was. When Jonah-Blue wasn't at the beach by himself – where he wasn't supposed to go alone but did all the time – Jonah-Blue would read book after book after book. Or he'd draw in his spiral notebook, which he kept hidden from me – I never got to see what he drew 'til he was gone. When I finally did get hold of his notebook, I wished I hadn't, but it helped me understand, sort of, a little better. I did throw his notebook into the trash bin at the end of the beach access path after I looked through it; neither Mama or Oma or anyone else needed to see what Jonah-Blue had put into those pages.

Mama would take us to the library once a week, and when we got home, Jonah-Blue would sometimes stay in the car and read and not even come out until his first book was finished. Then Mama would get mad and tell Jonah-Blue to take himself out into the fresh air this instant young man. Jonah-Blue would just take his next book and walk outside with it and start reading again.

When Jonah-Blue was at the house but wasn't reading or drawing, he was playing with his one toy, an old glass terrarium he had found in the twenty-five-cent box at an estate sale we had gone to with Oma Thiele. Jonah-Blue once kept miniature toads in his terrarium; he fed them tiny red ants. But our cat knocked the terrarium over and set the frogs free. They jumped their itty-bitty hearts out to everlasting freedom; we couldn't blame them for doing that. That summer, after the frogs had escaped, Jonah-Blue turned his terrarium into an enchanted lagoon. He filled the terrarium with water and added a smidge of blue food colouring and one drop of green. That, he said, created a barrier wreath effect. Jonah-Blue would then sift a handful of sand into the bowl, which would settle to the bottom. That became the sea floor. Next, he would draw mermaids, usually two of them; one was a boy, a merman, and one would be a girl, a woman. He would cut them out, like paper dolls. They were grown-up mer-people, with their proper private parts. Jonah-Blue never let real grown-ups see them. When we were alone at the house, Jonah-Blue would drop the paper figures into the pale-coloured water of his terrarium. He then would take the eraser end of one of his school pencils and push the mermaids around in the water, making them dance and bend and bob until the ink dissolved and their paper shapes turned to mulch and floated to the top, like dirty sea foam on the beach after a storm. The whole, pulpy mess he'd then just dump into the toilet and the weird game was over.

There were two reasons why Jonah-Blue played this paper game when our mother was out: First, Mama once told him that mermaids were for girls. We suspect Mama was just thinking of that stupid cartoon movie mermaid with all that red hair, but we both knew better than that. Jonah-Blue told me all about Neverland's mean and nasty mermaids, and he also told me about sirens – not the wailing things up-top of ambulances, but women who sang to sailors, who bewitched them, and made their ships crash on the rocks, making the sailors die. Jonah-Blue showed me a picture in volume six of his set of books called, "Legends & Lore from A to Z." It was a super old illustration of a very ugly, dog-faced mermaid with saggy boobs, in the chapter called, "On Ancient Sea Creatures & Monsters of the Deep." No, I agreed with my brother, these mermaids were definitely not girly-girl things, and they definitely weren't always meant for kids. When Jonah-Blue played his paper mermaid game, it made us feel a little a little naughty, which made us feel a little grown-up.

The main reason why Jonah-Blue kept his paper mermaids a secret was that he drew them naked. Jonah-Blue's mermaids were not covered up with big, dopey scallop shells or bikini tops. That, he said, was stupid and small-minded. Jonah-Blue's naked mermaids were mysterious to both of us, as neither one of us were too sure what naked grown-ups, let alone naked mermaids, looked like. We'd caught glimpses of our mother here and there, and of course I knew my body and Jonah-Blue knew his; we both could still remember playing in the sprinkler without any bathing suits on when we were really young. But, as we were only eleven that summer, there wasn't a whole heck of a lot else to see or to know – not yet anyway, as far as either one of us could tell about the other. So, Jonah-Blue's mermaid bodies wound up being part stolen-glance fantasy, part science, and part wondering. But Jonah-Blue sure liked to draw that stuff; and, sure, I liked to watch. But I thought it was funny and liked it best when their bodies turned to mush. That's where we were different; for me, it was all about silly, melting characters. For Jonah-Blue, it wasn't silly; it was something else – I just don't know what.

Jonah-Blue could do one other thing really well,

and that was swim. He said he wanted to be a marine biologist someday, doing research or something along those lines, so long it was in the ocean. Jonah-Blue would often have me time him holding his breath – he said if he didn't feel like going to college, he could become a professional free-diver. That freaked me out – why ever would someone want to go way, way down into the ocean, holding on to dear life with one single puff of breath in their lungs?

Being that we lived on the beach, like I said, Rule Number One was to never, ever go into the ocean without adult supervision. So we went into the ocean by ourselves all the time. As I loved to swim too and could hold my own against the waves, I had no problem breaking Rule Number One alongside my brother. We swam in the ocean when it was too cold, we swam in the ocean when it was too choppy, and we swam in the ocean when the jellyfish swarmed and warning signs with pictures of jellyfish with red slash marks over them were stuck in the sand all over the beach. We loved best to swim in the ocean, the "salty beach," as Jonah-Blue called it when he was little, when most other humans didn't want to be there.

Sometimes hurricanes, hundreds of miles out, would churn up the ocean floors, and the tides would throw up all kinds of clean, new shells from the ocean floors and toss them onto our beach. Those were our best times at the beach, when we could gather seashells like Easter eggs, left there just for us. Naturally, we had baskets and baskets full of seashells. On rainy days, I would sort them into collections and pretend to sell them to my dolls. When the hurricanes stewed and the beaches were empty, it felt like the world belonged to us. The shore was endless because it had no fences; neither did our grassy, sandy back yard. The endless, big, big empty ocean was, I thought, ours too.

When we snuck out to the beach, Jonah always cut through the breaking waves and swam far out beyond shore, farther than I'd ever dare go. He'd swim out so far, his head would look like nothing more than a brown apple seed on the waves, bobbing up and down, and sometimes disappearing altogether. Since I was only a few minutes older than him, it wasn't my place to scold him and tell him to stay closer to shore. If he wanted to swim around like some daredevil, that was his business. It was kind of cool, anyways; to have a sort-of-twin who was so unafraid. Sometimes – I'm not sure though – it would look like another apple seed would appear, even farther out than Jonah-Blue's. It would look like another swimmer was way, way out there with him. I always figured it was a stray buoy or my eyes playing tricks on me. Jonah-Blue never said anything about that other apple seed in the water. He never said he saw anyone out there; but then, he didn't usually have all that much to say about anything.

As I already told you, Jonah-Blue could hold his breath for a super long time, much longer than anyone I have ever known. He would dive under the waves and appear super far from where he had started, never minding the salt in his eyes or nose. Jonah-Blue once told me he could see underwater, that his retinas worked like camera lenses. I almost believed him, because he'd tell me what he saw on the ocean floor, even when it was way past either of us being able to stand in the water. Jonah-Blue's long eyelashes, when they were wet, even looked to me like the spines of tiny black sea urchins – so much about him was about the ocean. I might have been the blond haired, brown-eyed sister with the bright-coloured energy, but my brother had been the blue baby, with blue feelings and blue-green-coloured eyes. We were each matched up to our true colour selves. I was a garden, and Jonah-Blue was the sea.

After he was gone, I would sometimes wonder what

my brother had been doing on land all those years.

It was a Thursday, about a week after the last hurricane to come through, almost but not quite making landfall. We had seen some great shells on the beach the last couple of days, and Jonah-Blue and I got busy gathering up the best ones and throwing them into our buckets. Jonah-Blue had decided we ought to make a tidal pool behind the boulders. He had read, the sea was our last resource and wanted to see how it would work to have an ocean-garden to take care of, much as our Oma had her vegetable garden.

A tidal pool near the boulders seemed like the perfect way to set about our project. It was an out of the way spot and hard to get to, in a place pretty much left alone by all those pesky, pussyfooted tourists. Jonah-Blue decided on a small, natural trough behind some boulders, on a berm near the shore, which you could only get to by climbing up and over this craggled row of sharp rocks we called our jungle gym. We dug and dug and dug, hands and shovels. When we were done digging, we lined the hole solid with all the best mussels, oyster and clam shells we had gathered for our project. We worked for a long time, arranging and re-arranging the seashells, adding rocks as we needed them. When our pool was done, it was really more a grotto, practically fit for a Mer-King. Or a Mary, Mary, quite contrary, how does your garden grow sort of grand bath, silver bells and cockle shells and pretty maids all in a row....

The next morning, this thing called the Perigean Spring Tide was supposed to have come in and filled our tide pool water garden. This extra little-bit-higher tide only happened ever so often; Jonah-Blue seemed to know when to expect it. He said it had to do with the moon lining up with other stuff, also being when the moon was full, which it had been. I know that much for sure, because the moon had been extra bright that night; it had woken me up from my sleep. I remember looking out my window and seeing Jonah-Blue, awake as usual while everyone else was asleep, standing at the edge of our yard where it met up with the dunes, where the grass changed to sand, staring out over the ocean, into the face of the biggest moon I'd ever seen. He sure did look blue that night, out there in all that blue light.

That Thursday started up as an especially windy day; I guess the Spring Tides whip the air around with them, too. Jonah-Blue said we needed to hurry, so right after breakfast we ducked out – mom had left for work and our Oma was only expecting us at lunch time, so we had the morning to ourselves. Jonah-Blue dashed off the back porch and I followed, carrying my bucket of shells.

The breeze caught my hair up hard and tangled it across my forehead so I could hardly see where I was going; it also caught in my mouth, so I could hardly say a thing. I was having trouble keeping up with Jonah-Blue, who in his blue-energy was all about that ocean garden, and way ahead of me. My bucket was over half full and pretty heavy with our last batch of shells, some awesome cones and cockles big as teacups. I couldn't keep up with him and fell behind, he was going so fast. I almost felt left out. When I called his name, wanting to ask him to slow down, the wind took the words right out of my mouth and threw them in the opposite direction. Jonah never heard me.

When I finally came around the first boulder, the biggest one of all, I could see my brother again.

He was standing as still as a statue, his eyes as wide as I'd ever seen them, and they weren't blinking, either. His mouth was open too, frozen, not in an "Oh," but an "Ah." I followed his eyes to where they were looking, and I took a few steps closer. I really needed to see what the heck had made him freeze up like that.

That was when I first saw her. Or it. No, it was a her;

definitely a her.

There was the tide pool. Our beautiful shell-lined ocean garden, as long as I was tall, and about half that wide. The pool was pretty deep; we'd dug long and hard, so the shallow trough by the boulders was now the size of a bathtub. The water from the surge of the Tide had filled our pool to the brim; it was as clear in there as the water in Jonah-Blue's terrarium. The prettiest shells we had used to line the top edge of the pool, so it looked almost like a fancy bed, all framed with scallops and cockles. Dark seaweed had washed in with the water and floated on the surface, slick lace on a mirror. We could see ourselves. Everything looked like it ought to, like what we had made, like what I would have expected, but for this person, this girl who was lying on the bottom of our pool, under the water, face up. Our pool.

This girl was resting on her back, on our blanket of shells, looking straight at Jonah-Blue. I could see her blink – blinking at Jonah-Blue? – just like anyone would normally blink. She did it again, still staring at my brother. Then she did it again. This girl, lying there on the bottom of our pool, our ocean-garden, with about two feet of water over her, was as still as the water, but for her blinking eyes. The seaweed, slinking so slowly around on the top, shaped itself into a slimy wreath over her head. It mixed with curls of her hair that had floated up. Weird crown. Lying where she did, her waist was at about where the floor of our pool started to curve up to the berm, where my brother and I were standing. Up along the inside of the pool, it wasn't a pair of legs that rested on the slope, but a huge, blue-gray tail. The tail was draped over our pool's edge; it curled around, it did not bend like our legs might bend; there was nothing that would make anyone think there was a pair of knees inside.

Up and over the edge of our pool and onto the sand trailed the rest of this girl. Her smooth – *body?* – tapered off and ended in what was obviously a set of fins. These fanned out as wide as my arms could reach stretch, end to end. They were shaped like two harps, facing away from each other. The fins were frosty-clear; skinny spines shone through, and they flashed in all the colors of an abalone shell, all the colors you could ever wish to find: silver, blue, green, gold, pink. Wow, was she creepy. Creepy but awesome, creepy but gorgeous.

This – this *omigosh could she be a real, live mermaid* – girl just lay there, super relaxed, super still beneath the water, but for this tap, tap, tap she did with her tail on the sand, just as any one of us might tap our fingernails on our desktops at school. Her crazy, amazing tail tapped the ground, flashing its colours, keeping time with something I suppose only she could hear. And each time her fins hit the wet sand the whole thing jingled; because, you see, dozens and dozens of earrings were pierced through the tailfins' edges. The earrings – and not a single one of them matched any other – twinkled in the sun, making the sound of a hundred tiny bells every time the fins hit the sand. Me, being a kid who also happened to like jewellery, knew right away what this was: This was a collection of earrings, lost by swimmers and boaters, which had been gathered up in just the same way Jonah-Blue and I collected our seashells. The girl saw me staring at her tail and all those earrings, and she smiled. She understood that thing about wanting to wear pretty stuff.

She then looked back over again at Jonah-Blue. I swear I saw her face change. Her eyes, almond-shaped, with their long, white eyelashes, blinked at him again, and the smile she smiled was of the melting kind that you only give someone you care a whole heck of a lot about. What a bunch of baloney, I thought when I caught myself thinking that; I had watched too many old romance movies with Oma Thiele for my own good. Here I was, turning a freaky-amazing discovery into what my Grandmother called yet another mellow-drama, whatever that was.

Jonah-Blue dropped his bucket on the ground. It landed on its side and the shells spilled out. He didn't notice. Like some spell-bound Prince who had just discovered his Sleeping Beauty or, better yet, his Snow White. I wanted to gag. Sure, the girl was pretty, even if she was so pale, even if her lips were purplish, and even if she did have a tail that looked more like a dolphin's – a dolphin with a pierced-up, punked-out fish's tail. The girl with her tail looked endlessly long and skinny, shiny and sleek. She had all the good looks any girl on land would have been tickled pink to have, with one of those heart-shaped faces too, but for the fact she had no legs or feet, which was kind of gross at first sight. What hair of hers wasn't floating in curly-Qs with the seaweed on the top of the pool was braided into a long, fat ponytail and wound around her neck like a scarf. The human-girl thing, about wanting to wear pretty things, was obvious there too: I saw it in all the jagged coral beads strung through her hair; like strands of cranberries, they were twisted in and out through her braid.

The girl started to play with her ponytail as her eyes moved back and forth between us. She was studying us, comparing us, trying to figure out who we were to each other. She looked to be about our age; didn't look much older than either Jonah-Blue or me. I mean, well, maybe max a year or two older, at least in human years, because she already had little round boobs that sat on top of her skinny ribcage, while I was still as flat as a board. Yep, she had ribs and a bellybutton and arms and hands just like me, but that was about it. There was one thing I noticed right away, what was different about her body from mine, was that it was totally, I mean, completely motionless. Her ribs and her belly didn't move in the way ours do when we breathe: In, out, in, out, in out, up and down. That's because, naturally, she wasn't breathing. She didn't breathe – only land people, like me and my almost-twin brother, did that.

The girl, who seemed to be reading my face and my eyes and practically my mind, then turned her face away from me and lifted her ponytail. Behind her pointed ear I could see three, feather-edged, bright red slits, edged in the same blue as her tail. Gills.

A mermaid. A real, honest to God mermaid. Our mermaid. The mermaid saw that I finally got it.

She smiled. I thought I knew, right at that very moment, we would all be best friends forever.

The best.

The mermaid in our tide pool turned her eyes back on Jonah-Blue, who had now gotten to his knees at the edge of the pool. There, I saw it again, her whole face changing when she was looking at my brother. Everything went soft. My tummy tickled and my heart skipped a beat. All of a sudden, I felt left out again, and also afraid. I would not have been able to tell you why at that moment, though later I could have.

My brother leaned forward – way, way forward. His ocean eyes stayed on the mermaid's even paler ones. They were frozen, hypnotised: a boy on the sand and a girl under a couple feet of water, staring at each other, sending something – thoughts, feelings, magic, who knows – between them, which I couldn't read. I guess I was never meant to. I was not a part of It. The energy of what was happening, whatever It was I could sense, was strong. So strong, It separated me from them, without me budging one single inch. It was like they had known each other for a long time but had never had a chance to actually say *Hi*.

They were already holding hands with their eyes.

In the next fraction of a second, with the power of a hooked marlin breaking up and out of a wave, the sea maiden leapt out of the water, sending salted droplets flying and blinding the sister's eyes with the force of their sting. In a super-human manoeuvre, the mermaid hovered, bolt upright, and wrapped her slender arms around the boy, who remained in his trance. With the speed and grace of a constricting python, she drew him deep into her embrace.

But this was no mere embrace; this was a capture, and the boy was her willing hostage.

The boy continued to melt, farther into the circle of the mermaid's strong arms. The boy's sister gasped audibly, too stunned to make any other noise. Her voice was gone, her lungs refusing to release the air they had grabbed with reflexive, survivalist desperation. The sister stood, rooted to the ground, the only firmament she and her brother had known as theirs until that day, her white knuckled hands still clenching the handle of her bucket. She was holding on for dear life.

The mermaid leaned in and kissed the boy, who in that instant was no longer a child, an almost-twin brother, the son of an overworked, single mother. He, who was no longer a child, kissed the mermaid-girl back, with an innocent passion so devoid of showmanship and masculine bravado, that what he returned was, by all standards of seduction and promise and hunger, a perfect kiss.

The mermaid next raised her right hand, her index finger outstretched, for an infinitesimal moment. She brought her hand down and across in an arc with such speed her action was but a blur. What happened in that blur was that the mermaid's fingernail, a razor-sharp, serrated talon, met with the boy's neck, just below his right ear, where she cut a deep gash into his flesh.

Before the boy's sister could even think to muster a scream, the mermaid repeated her attack, slicing crossways to cut another gash into the other side of the boy's neck, right below his left ear. Blood, after the body's momentary shock, streamed from the wounds in two garnet-coloured ribbons, ever brighter against his fading skin. The boy opened his mouth to cry out in pain but was quickly stilled with a second, deep kiss from his captor. As the mermaid held his mouth with hers, she pressed her bony hands against his neck to stop the flow of blood, which had already formed a dark pool in the sand at his feet, her tail.

The mermaid pulled free from the kiss, a water-bound vampire coming up for air. The boy exhaled long, long, long. Deeply, and finally.

The mermaid turned her head just enough to looked around and meet once more the eyes of the boy's hapless, fear-paralyzed sister. Her pale eyes said: *Thank you, and I know you understand, because you will soon feel like I do, though right now, you don't.* The mermaid's eyes then also said: *But I don't care what you think, because I have been waiting for this longer than you will ever know.*

So, I guess I'm sorry if I scared you, but your broken heart isn't going to change anything. You don't get to get to keep this one.

He is mine now.

The mermaid turned back to study her companion, tenderly assessing his condition, pressing him to her. The flow from the wounds in the boy's neck slowed to a trickle, oozing only occasional droplets. The boy still clung to his willowy succubus in a fully drowning state of – something. He looked bewildered, but not frightened. His expression was full of feeling, but he did not convey anything even remotely associated with pain; at least, not any longer. She stroked the hair out of the boy's eyes, pleased to see the last whispers of any mortal breath fully eradicated from within her companion.

One second, one epoch after that, the mermaid sprang to action. With a single, powerful thrust of her tail, she catapulted herself and the boy into the air in a graceful arc, which, as it turned out, was perfectly timed to coincide with the overhead explosion of a rogue ocean wave, which washed over them all, droplets crashing wet diamonds around them. The surge from the wave that followed lifted the pair, hurling them deep into the massive rush of its crest. As it did so, the almost-twin sister was pushed aside and knocked to the ground.

In a grand splash, the two were gone, and the girl sat alone.

The girl, the big sister, the almost-twin, sunk into the sand, beyond tears, beyond crying out. When a fairytale unfolds before your very eyes, it is not necessarily a pretty thing. It can, in fact, be a rather grim, even gruesome event.

Andersen be damned.

INSIDE OUT
by Grace Reynolds

Mark Dillon felt a sense of freedom standing on the top of Carr Peak in the Huachuca Mountains of Arizona. He had hiked this trail at least a dozen times since the U.S. Army stationed him in the nearby town of Sierra Vista. Every time he made the trek up the mountain, he felt like a giant among men. Whenever the grunt life was getting to him, he always knew he could look forward to that hike to get away from the base, even if it was just for an afternoon.

Mark didn't have much money to his name, especially at the less-coveted rank of Specialist. The cost of living in Arizona was fortunately lower than that of other duty stations across the United States. At least here he didn't have to struggle as much to pay the bills and, lucky for him, most of the gear he could ever need for camping or hiking was provided to him free of charge for training purposes. A kid from

Michigan that was used to brutal winters, Mark had welcomed Arizona's hot summers. Sure, the temperatures could get well over one hundred degrees Fahrenheit in the summertime but, hey, it was a dry heat. The hot air was more tolerable in Arizona than in other parts of the country, where the humidity would leave you sopping wet as soon as you walked out the front door.

Carr Peak, the third tallest mountain in the state of Arizona, was home to a large array of plant and animal life. Incredible geographic features such as the beautiful limestone cliffs and natural waterfalls were on full display. Today was one of the hotter days, clocking in at one hundred and three. While the climb up may have been a bit harder because of the heat, Mark knew that the trip back down the mountain would be a breeze. He took it all in; the gorgeous views of Cochise County spread before him and to the south, he could just make out the grassy plains of Mexico. It was all so perfectly serene up here – but all that goes up must come down.

Mark heard a buzzing from the bushes nearby and stood still for a moment to listen. Feeling bold, he silently peered overhead to get a look at the creature just on the other side. He was met with an Arizonan vision that he had only dreamed of coming across out in the wild. Mark had a front row seat to a battle between a large, menacing tarantula and a nefarious tarantula hawk.

Despite its name, the tarantula hawk was neither tarantula nor hawk. It was, in fact, a prehistoric-looking wasp with amber wings and a complementary thorax and abdomen that had the most hauntingly beautiful blue sheen. The wasp had earned its name thanks to its reputation of hunting the largest type of spider to roam the earth.

Mark's buddy, Brady, back on the base had told him that the tarantula hawk would find its prey due to a chemical it could smell in the air signaling that a tarantula burrow was near. It would then scope out where the spider's nest was and provoke it out of its lair for a battle royale. Once instigated, the tarantula would lift its abdomen and display its fangs as a show of force to scare off the wasp... but that's exactly what the tarantula hawk was waiting for. It would quickly jab the underbelly of the furry beast with its long stinger, permanently immobilizing the creature.

That, however, wasn't the most sinister part of the tarantula hawk's attack. The real horror story was enveloped in the aftermath of the initial sting. While the tarantula lay there, unable to even writhe in all of its pain, the wasp would drag the undead carcass to its secret lair and lay an egg inside of the tarantula's abdomen. It would then bury the entrance to its hiding spot and the egg would eventually hatch a larva, who would then feast on the innards of the spider. Once the larva had matured into an adult, it would claw its way out of the tarantula's corpse, digging out from underground to emerge, ready to carry on its facinorous tradition of hunting and leaving its offspring to eat their prey from the inside out.

'Gnarly,' Mark whispered out loud. He had never seen a tarantula hawk in person and had to get a closer look. He pulled out his phone so he could record a video, but clumsily dropped the thing right next to the brawl before him. Unfortunately, the graceless fall of his phone had startled the tarantula, giving it a chance to run away from the human predator before it.

The tarantula hawk, however, was enraged and shifted its vicious stare in Mark's direction.

As the wasp crawled closer to Mark, the zizzing got louder. He had heard that, second only to the bullet ant, the tarantula hawk's sting was one of the most painful in the world. While they normally wouldn't attack humans, their stings had been known to temporarily immobilize a person for a couple of minutes. Mark looked at his phone lying on the ground and knew he had to get out of there, fast.

He looked at the bug and back at his phone, trying to perfectly time his reach to grab it. Maybe he could distract the tarantula hawk. He jumped to the right and the wasp followed. He hopped to the left and the wasp again repeated Mark's movement. He tried to trick the wasp and pretended to jump to the right but quickly shifted his body to the left for his phone.

A burning pain suddenly radiated through Mark's leg.

He had not been quick enough for the tarantula hawk. His fear was realised in a matter of milliseconds: he had been stung.

Mark cried out in excruciating pain and instinctively reached down for his leg but lost his balance and fell into a nearby shrub of cacti on the trail. 'Goddamnit!' He had landed perfectly on his back and felt the sharp stab of hundreds of acicular points in his arms, legs, and neck. With every wave of pain in his leg, his body shook further, providing uninterrupted suffering. Mark tried to control his breathing to keep himself from spiralling into complete panic. He was going to get himself out of this mess – at least, he hoped. He felt a light tapping on his vulnerable forearms.

Mark looked down – the tarantula hawk had returned, hissing and preparing to strike. 'NO, NO, NO, NO!' Mark howled as the insect pushed its abdomen forcefully into his skin. In a matter of moments, the wasp had immobilized both his leg and his arm. He wanted to break himself free but the waves of agony made him sick. Mark felt a surge of nausea overcome him but he fought off the urge to puke into the shrub in which he was now entangled.

His phone was still on the ground next to the pack that he now realized he had dropped, full of protein bars and his water supply for the hike. He had to get help somehow. The pain in his leg had begun to subside and he violently cried out for the virtual assistant on his phone. 'CALL BRADY!'

A wave of blue and pink lights danced on the screen of his phone. Seconds felt like minutes and he was afraid of the wasp returning.

'*Do you want me to call Stacey?*' a robotic voice replied.

'Fuck, no! CALL BRADY!' he screamed out again.

The colours danced again on the screen as it searched to fulfill Mark's request. '*Unable to make your call to Stacey.'*

'COME ON!'

Mark began screaming as loud as he could, hoping a fellow hiker would hear his voice and know he was in trouble. The only sound he had heard in reply were echoes of his own terrors carrying away into the canyon below him.

Mark heard the angry droning again.

Panic started to set in as Mark began to feel trapped up there on the mountain. If he could not lift, or even roll himself off this cactus he would probably be stuck here and die of heatstroke. Against all of his instincts, he willed his body to roll one side off of the cactus and summon the drive to somehow stand on one of his feet. He gritted his teeth and muffled his screams as he tried to bear down his anguish and pushed with all he had. He felt the needles of the cacti release from the back of his right arm as he turned towards his left. Deliverance was within his grasp!

But then he felt a sting to the back of his neck.

Shocked, Mark rolled over into the cacti on his stomach instead of breaking himself free as he had intended. What was worse than the sharp pang at the base of his skull was a throbbing in the front of his head; he saw blood trickling onto the dirt below him.

Cactus needles had impaled both of his eyes.

With every blink and unintentional shake of his corneas he felt the foregin objects lodging deeper toward his optic nerves. He began to vomit violently and started to choke on the thick green bile he was spewing onto the ground, sickened by his terrestrial trauma. As his impaired vision begun to fade to darkness he saw the ruthless wasp had started its final ascent to close in on him.

Slowly, the wasp creeped up to the barbed succulent. With what little sight he had left, Mark's eyes flared with fear as he focused in on the insect's vignette. The needles that had pierced his face left him unable to shake himself free and he knew he had been trapped; trapped like the tarantulas that the wasp had likely buried hundreds of times before. His eye winced and shed a tear as he gagged on leftover bile and pleas, but the tarantula hawk was bound to have its retribution.

Mark felt tiny feet pitter-pattering against his cheeks and they finally approached his lips, now crusted from an insatiable thirst in the desert heat. As he let out one last shriek, the wasp buried its stinger deep into the roof of his mouth, ceasing Mark's voice once and for all. Screams turned into involuntary retches and the tarantula hawk left its final grim blessing by planting a single egg against the dying soldier's palate.

The military base's Commanding General would begin his press conference in a matter of minutes. His hands were clammy and he looked out into the crowd. Nobody likes to deliver the sad news of a soldier's death, but it had to be addressed after a group of hikers found the remains of Specialist Mark Dillon skewered on a shrub of cacti at the top of Carr Peak.

The soldier had been missing for several weeks and no resource had been spared in searching for his whereabouts. Although Specialist Dillon's remains were located mere feet from a well-trafficked hiking trail, his body had been concealed by the variety of plant life that became his tomb. Alarmed by a wretched smell on a leisurely trip up the mountain, a group of horrified hikers alerted both law enforcement and the local news of their gruesome discovery. The grisly details of his death had been the talk of not just the town, but the nation. Everyone wanted answers.

Of course the General would tell the world the story

of Specialist Dillon's death – at least the one the Public Affairs Office carefully designed with the assistance of the town's medical examiner.

Specialist Dillon had experienced a heat stroke that had gone untreated. In his delirious state, he fell into the cacti and trapped himself. It was an unusually hot day and after failed attempts to call someone for help or reach his water supply, Specialist Dillon tragically died of dehydration.

The General would not reveal, however, that Specialist Dillon's body had been found in an advanced state of decay, or that the hikers had found a solitary tarantula hawk feasting on the inside of his half-eaten mandible. No, he would not tell everyone that Mark had suffered a more spine-chilling death than the tale their staff had crafted for the media.

He could not tell them that Specialist Mark Dillon, at the young age of twenty-two, was eaten alive from the inside out.

DESCENT

by Sarah Roberts and Michael Benavidez

The rat is back. At least, I think it's a rat. I haven't been able to touch it, but it touches me. It scuttles across the ground, pausing every three seconds. I imagine it's sniffing or doing whatever rodents do. The pace seems to slow as it gets closer. I can hear it sniffing when it's near my face. Always sniffing. It echoes in the silence of this place.

Oh, to think I'd miss it all. To think I'd long for the crick of crickets, the rustle of trees, and the world of sound and light. I wish I had never abandoned the midnight chorus. This world, this cavern, this new home has become topsy-turvy. It seems all has lost meaning to me, all sense gone. Down in this hole... or is it up in a cavernous cell? I no longer know where in this map of topography I roam. Left has become right, right into diagonal, and a day into ten. I am lost. All is lost without sun, without sound. Except for a rat, somewhere. It walks with sense and purpose, and sight that I do not have.

Where did the light go? When? How? Does it matter? I don't think so. I trampled up a cliff's side, ever an amateur explorer. There, I found a cave. And yes, within the cave there is only darkness, but the black did not meet me in the cave, it came before...

The sun, a ball of light and fire that seemed as mythical as the gods that made it, was being eclipsed. Mayhap it was the moon, but I doubt it so. I had seen many eclipses. I believe this was something more – something bigger, greater. I believe the sun was killed. It was not a slow transition, but immediate, and it burned my eyes to see, but stare I did. The winds grew still; an inhalation of sound seemed to puncture my eardrums deaf. There was no tinnitus ring. There was nothing. Only the breaking of my senses, as I nearly lost my grip on where I stood. To tumble down such a steep cliff, on such a dark silent night, with no one around to hear me, would I make a sound?

It did not matter because I did not fall. Instead, by some miracle, a guiding hand of God, I made it to the cave. I know it was a cave for when my foot stepped to reach across it fell in, and I with it, tumbling up into nothingness, where there was no light. But there were sounds, scuttling sounds. That damned rat.

I grow hungry.

There is no echo here. There is no echo, but still I hear my heavy breaths as I try and make my way to the wall of what is to be my mausoleum. I believe I have mistaken my position. I thought myself at the room's center, and thought to have moved to my left, to find a wall and follow it. Only now, I find that the movement has become more taxing the longer I go. Most in part because of my legs – the likes of which I question their being there or not – but also because there has come a steepness to this movement. I am going in a direction, and it is up. This joys me for a moment. Blind to where I'll go, blind to what will come, I know one thing. I'm going somewhere.

I crawl, what remains of my appendages dragging behind me. The legs had long given out on me, gone numb and dumb. I don't know why. I remember pain and a loud snap. That may have been me, but it was done and over with before I could register what it was.

I'm not sure how long I've been climbing. Feels like hours, now. At times it seems that my passage through this earthen hell veers back into the depths. Back to the rat. Then it shifts again to the heavens, the clean air, and the sunlight. There must be sunlight still.

Though it feels as if the whole world has gone dark, there must be sunlight!

What was that? The skuttle of nails. A scamper. A rat? No. *The* rat! It follows me. It's waiting for me to falter so it can feast on my skin. I've felt it sniffing with that twitchy nose. They all want a piece! Well, they can come and get it. I can't imagine there is much of me left anyway. Even less when the rat finishes with me.

I'm certain now that this corridor goes up just as it goes down. If I can find a rock, something to mark my path, my suspicions may be confirmed.

Ah-ha! Here's something. A long, surprisingly light rock with a smooth surface. It will do the trick. I will set it up against the wall to my right and then continue on.

On and on and on and...

Time contorts. I feel as though I am in rewind, and fast forward. My legs sometimes feel as though they are there; other times I know they are not. I hold my breath to count the time, knowing that as a child I could hold for a full minute and change, but within what feels like a second I am withered and done. Was that a second, or was that a minute? What does that say about a day, a year...

I have not fed. I have not drank. I have not pissed or

shat. My body is empty and still I thrive. What is this madness? What has become of me?

There, I see something there. A far view, a mirage – must be. Remembrance is a cruelty for the human mind when it has nothing else. Having nothing to spare but further time, or lack thereof, I slither to it. A shining glitter in the aftermath of darkness. It distorts, it shifts shapes and churns in my eyes. It hurts. I think to close my eyes, but don't know how anymore. There hasn't been a need to. I get to it: a pond with an echo.

A pond! With an echo!

I'd shout vulgarities of pleasure if I could think to use my mouth. I don't remember what it's like to speak, or drink. What do I do? How do I do? Never mind that, I go forward onto it, to bathe in its colour, crystal clear blue. But what I see, what I see with pained eyes scares me.

I see me.

I have devolved into something beyond, or beneath, what I once was. Adapting, they call it. Mutations take years. How long have I suffered? My mouth and cheeks have drooped, and hang low beneath my chin – that too has changed into a sunken feature that merges with my neck. I lift the lips and check. What has become of me? My fingers are long; extra knuckles have turned them into raked claws, fingernails gone and, in their place, sharpened callouses to make use of as a grip. The teeth, my teeth, are no more. My gums are rotted and grey as the skin that covers me. I look as though I am of the undead.

My body has sagged and bloated, each exhale turning me into a sluggish sight that could slip into the easiest cracks. Every inhale turning me into a blob creature. My legs, ha! What legs? They must have gone long ago, and in their place is nothing. No nubs, no knee, no trailing remnants. I assume they rotted long ago and whatever entrails were left have merely gone off in their time, leaving me with a flat end for my excess skin to cover.

And my eyes! They nearly do not exist. Skin grows over them. I peer through slits unblinking. There are no eyelids, no eyebrows, no hair, no anything. I am no longer a man. In anguish, I jump myself into the pool.

I am an abomination, and must drown.

I squirm into it, feeling the coolness of it burn my skin, ever so sensitive. And if I had the ability to weep, then, I would. My perception has been poor. This pool with its echo is no such thing. It is a puddle. A stray puddle, the last of its kind. And it is absorbed into my skin before I can plant my face into it.

I cannot die.

I spasm upwards. I hit the ceiling and collapse onto the floor. I search myself for my deformities, but am so lost in my dread and this cave and my own self that my hands cannot recognize my own features anymore.

Do I dream? Could this be just that – a dream? A nightmare? Delirium catches me, a sweet release from the darkness. In it, I swim an ocean of pulsing green light. The waves of its illness threaten to take me under, but I stroke and stroke until my lips find their way to the surface. I suck in the air in hungry gulps. So hungry. Desperate. Longing. My lungs burn. They ache for nourishment even more than my stomach. Each gasping suck of air fills me, feeding my blood with the life they need to go on.

But what is the point? Why bother? I'm drowning here. Drowning in darkness. Drowning in hunger. Drowning in my own filth and despair. What has become of me in this endless living nightmare? Am I lost in a cavern? Am I? Or is this my hell, my purgatory? I can't imagine what I could have done in life to deserve this!

Except, maybe...

Fuck them. Fuck all of them. Not that they drowned. Not that they sank into a pit of black and nothing and *this fucking rat*! It's here! It's with me and won't let me be!

I will eat its heart before the devils take me!

I pull with all the strength left in me to find the wall. Leaning into it, I suck deep the stale air. For a moment I think myself alone in this madness, but then the skuttle.

It taunts me, my gaunt rodent. Its movements slow with mine, so much so that I am finally able to grab it, but only for a moment. Long enough to feel its loose skin and bony protrusions. Long enough for the wretched bastard to sink its teeth into my hand like all of the other bitey things.

I fling it then with all I have, aiming for what I hope is another wall in the dark. There is no sound. No thump or squeak. I pull myself to the spot and reach with bloody hands into the abyss. Nothing. No wall. No rat.

I'm sure there was a wall.

Circled this cell I have for countless days and each pass gave way to a wall; cold and definite. More solid than even the blackness that swallows me. Reaching, I probe the void.

With travel and exploration come new feelings. I grow hungry. Hungrier with every tick-tocking scurry of my companion. Come to me, friend. I won't hurt you again. I was angry – a short burst – I meant no ill will. Come, I am hungry, I won't hurt you. Show me where you feed, what you feed upon.

Nothing.

That bastard. That rat bastard has left me!

I've been abandoned. I've been left alone to my own insistent thoughts of what was, what is, and what could be. Ha! What could be? What could be does not matter to me, for I cannot see the product of such a sight. I am blind! And now, I am alone. I am left in such solitary confinement with nothing more than my thoughts and prayers, a useless fuckery of all that is left for me to indulge in.

I make to laugh, and to follow that laughter into a cry. I make no sound. Either I have gone deaf, and perhaps my friend has not gone away from me as I thought, or I've gone mute as well as blind. Should this cause panic in me? Panic seems to have retired itself to an unused part in my mind, for I feel nothing.

In a fury I punch a wall – only there is no wall, and I fall over. The fall seems to take ages. I travel down, down, down. Or so I think. In this hellish realm I may as well be falling up, up, up. And I think perhaps that may be true, for when I make impact, it's on my back.

We can thank the gods that while my sight and hearing and speech have all suffered a loss, my ability to feel pain has not. I think I have broken a limb or two. An attempt to stand up straight results in a new topple, as well as a feeling that my new surroundings have a rather short roof. I have gone from the wide reachings of the dark to the claustrophobic sanctuary of a new disaster.

I think I shall explore a bit more.

I think. I think...

There is an evil here and it has a name, but will not share it with me. It refuses to speak, to introduce itself to the fellow damned. But it's there, it lingers, a wanton presence that seeks to provoke me. I feel it, breathing on my neck, shifting its weight on my back when it thinks I sleep. But, fool that it is, it does not realise that I do not sleep!

I seek to catch it, this wraith that seeks to drive me mad. I grab at the dark, throwing my body over the floor as though a slug. Something slips across the remains of my legs; I feel it touch an exposed nerve. A stab of pain hits me, and I keep it in mind, ready to payback its trespasses onto me in full.

The son of a bitch toys with me, tickling a slab of muscle that holds one leg onto me. With all my strength, I push and throw my body up into a U-turn spin at the creature. It is fast – must be fast – for I miss and land on a leg. In anger I grab it and throw it into the dark, after my spectre. Forgotten that it was still a part of me, I faint as it snaps and runs after the evil in the dark.

What is this new sensation? What part of me? Do the parts discarded still feel, still beat with life? I feel so much less than I was and yet more. So much more. The pinpricks come in waves of glass shards lodged deep followed by dog hairs inserted just under the skin on the soles of my feet. Except I have no feet. What I wouldn't give for a dog... This new sensation travels. It leaves behind a trail of itch and stick. Thin threads of spun sugar. It clings to me, pulling in tighter as my skin ebbs and flows over my twitching bones. I feel the presence of another. Many others. But not the rat. My dearest friend... I manage to budge and feel my right side break free. There is a flurry of movement across my skin like the feet of a thousand tiny soldiers retreating at the bugle call. Lilliputians? Am I a giant trapped in a tiny world? A stranger in a stranger land. Twenty thousand leagues under the ground. The daggers pierce my flesh and a surge of acid boils through my blood as magma through volcanic vents. I try to scream.

There is no sound here.

It's caught in my exhalation and we both suffer fright. One of the damned fights my breath – many-legged, it holds to my lips. Too late, the stranger becomes acquainted with my mouth. A crunch later and I feel myself struggle free of their casings before more can befall the same fate, or worse... they become aware of the loss of their kin.

I am not fully able to escape the creatures; the fast little fuckers have set to work on me, in me. Where the skin hangs loose, they tunnel in and make their homes within me, blistered huts I'm sure. How long until their eggs hatch? Will it hurt? Will it tickle? Will I care?

Swearing to myself brings me little joy; the senses that I had thought were damned and gone – a good riddance to them, I didn't need them anyway in this spectacular establishment that was always willing to extend my reservation – seem to be returning.

The sound of one foot stomping teases me, the ghost of a ratty friend taking ride on the stump as it sweeps past me in such low tunnels. I feel its breeze tickle me, a musky scent of damp and rot urging me to turn back. But I will not. The babes on my back needed a fresh home from which to escape their parent's devouring, and I need to teach those no-good traitors it is not okay to tease the handicapped. Especially when I am only handicapped because the forgotten thing refused to return to me! And so I struggle on, feeling the drip, drop, drip of moisture flooding me with sweat.

What if this swelling in my chest is not love?

My babies grow. They feed from me; a small price to pay for their affection. These are my true kin. These are my blood. Not that treacherous rat; may it rot in the depths of this fucking hell never to see the light of day! Certainly none of those philandering, felonious, phalanges that so eagerly scurried away along with my untrue appendage. And after so many years together... Alas! I care not for things lost or things taken, for now I have a thousand limbs and on them I move through the dark in exploration of this fetid world.

How deep must this place be? It is but a hillside, and yet as I explore, ever blind, the passageways tunnel infinitely, scouring the underside flesh of the earth. Am I an all-too-familiar creature, making a home under the skin of the world, draining her of her nutrients to die. Or is this world already dead, and I but a wandering carrion bird pecking and insisting upon a corpse?

I crawl deeper, as I always do.

Noises alert me, and they sound of haunts from a life long gone. My mansion is invaded by these ghosts; wisps of whispers echo to me, unseen, unremembered, calling noises that linger on the edge of familiarity. Words, they are calling out words – but not just any words; a name! They call a name, one that caresses my wrinkled brain in the broken skull of a dying survivor. There is only one answer to this. Madness! I have gone mad! How long ago did this insanity come, and I not know of it? Barely now, in this joke too far, do I come to embrace the lunacy that must have taken me in. I must be mad. The voices call my name. It is my name they call! Monsters tempting me with memories that I had left many years ago when I was whole. Angry at the madness, I crawl at my fastest. On winged hands I fly! They dare try and make this life worse! I'll show them. I'll show these hallucinations the true extent of my madness!

These tunnels twist and turn like the flashes of a life no longer mine, carried on whispers that echo against the stone as they do my mind. My legs carry me forward. Hundreds of them; thin bent needles puncture the rock, lifting my body into the air. The voices come again. So familiar. So close. Shrill. Demanding. Who do they think they are to summon me? From the depths of this earthen hell I call my beasties to swarm, and soon the voices will feel my presence. They will feel my darkness and they will know my hell!

The mad fury dissents into something less. I feel my mind pulse and shiver, afraid. It warns me of what is ahead, but no. The command has been given. Fury dissipated but madness fully alive, I swim through the tunnel and curve into – my eyes! Oh, the agony! What fucked creature, imagined or not, would dare carry the sun in their palms? And more, how dare they drag it down into the depths of my home? Offenders!

The horror of its suddenness, of its piercing glare, brings forth a piercing shriek from my own self. So unnatural is my own voice to me, my own heart stutters. In all my years I have only ever heard the heavy breaths of my own work. But then there comes a second shriek, one much different than my own, and I work to fix myself better.

The sun flies down and around a tunnel curve, and I wish it would die a beautiful supernova. Out of sight and out of my mind. The creature continues its mouth calls; these are not words as I remember them. They are screams, I think. Whatever they may be, its owner continues ululating them and I follow its voice. While I move forward, it sets into a backwards run. But it will not escape me ever so easily. This thing has invaded my home; it will feel my bites.

With acute precision, I tackle it down. I did not have the chance to set my hands upon it, to silence its wretched noises – its echoes hurt my ears, my head pounds for it to stop, and have it stop I would! – when I hear it gasp, choke, and grow silent.

I feel it.

The creature is big, bigger than me as I stand. There is a face! Smaller than my own, a chin that is not moulded into its neck. What peculiar structure. I follow it down and find limbs, by god this creature has four! With legs whole, and fingers longer than eroded stubs, it's a fucking mutant! Something on it shakes; the whole body quivers, a light – more ghastly fucking light! – glows through the loose folds of skin, and shows its face. Eyes! The thing still has eyes! Wider than slits, but empty of intelligence.

In the distance, further noise. Voices, words, more! They do not call mine this time, they call another. But they will not find it, nor will they find me. My pets grab hold of it with me, tie it to myself. Together we haul the beastie into depths they would never explore. I alone know this place – twists and turns, we dig into the rocks.

It will be my new friend, and unlike the others it will not abandon or mutiny, for I will hold on to it and never let go.

In the darkness it cries. Begging sobs, epitaphs of its virtues, promises of rewards unwanted and undeliverable. It blathers on, relentless in its self-serving soliloquies. Why won't it just be quiet? This thing that was to be my pet is my curse. The bitey ones whisper to cut out its tongue. They are young, impatient. Hungry. I, too, hunger. But the tongue will remain. For now.

I think I will start with the skin. Cut it slow and thin. Just a sliver. A shaving. Tasty treat. The bitey ones tie it tight so it can't wriggle. I wonder if the face skin tastes different from that of the arm or the thigh? Salty, chewy. Oh, but the cheeks, they are so soft and sweet!

It screams more now.

The noise, the noise, the noise. Does it ever stop? The fucking noise! I'll go mad, I swear I will!

I beat on its face, the monstrous face. Juicy and sweet, now tenderized. It's quiet now. So quiet, nice quiet. Feeling its face I find it rounder than before, and can only hope it does not explode. Pop goes the weasel! What does a weasel look like again? Perhaps like the creature I've taken pet. My pet weasel.

It's trainable, I learn. Now its cries are soft, whimpered, pathetic little beggings. I leave it be, dragging it along with me wherever I may roam. For now... until I can find a way to peel it like a fresh fruit, juicy fruit so succulent I can taste it in my mouth.

Dare I press harder? This jagged edge cuts the flesh with an eagerness like that of my little beasties. How much pressure can the flesh take before it pops? I push. Firm but slow. I feel the give and the resistance. A little further... ah! The pop and spray. Warm, rich, metallic wetness hits my lips. A heat swells within me as I penetrate further, consumed by the intoxicating sensation of twitching, wet flesh around my fingers. Yes, scream for me, my darling. Scream for mercy for I know not what this word means. Scream for pity. I'll show you the same shown to me. But not before I engorge myself on your tender meat.

I lap at the fountain, panting heavy and greedy, bathe in it, let it soak and soil the earth with its pollutants. My beasties flee from the drips, but I roll in them. The cries turn to whimpers and then silence.

No! That will not do! Overexcited perhaps, I feast where I did not cut, and it screams. Yes joyous yes, music! It's a symphony, and I dance under its rain. I applaud, and drag it down with me, further down. Down where I hear retired friends chastise me. Bastards, jealous creatures that stomp and slither about as though they have any *right* to chastise me! I've my beasties! My friend and food and drink! And they have the darkness, lonesome maddening darkness. To silence their reverberating bullshit, I throw them the finger. Not mine, but its. The appendage rips easily – a tendon of flesh plays selfishly with my gift, but alas it gives! And give to the darkness it does, where they howl insult and go into hibernation. I have no need of them any longer. Satisfied, I lay on it, a wet – but soft – bed whose light-rising chest cradles and singsongs me to sleep. Easy sleep, where the world is less dark.

I wake with a start! A vision of my wrongness alarms me in full-detailed thought! Guilt, grief, they punish me my wrongs. I cry and cry into the open cavity of my bed fellow! Oh, I have done wrong! My dream has told me so! But what wrong? I... can't recall. It seems lost now. Head buried in it, I gnaw on a stone in it, pondering. What a mystery that moment was...

This beating heart calls to me, a voice so haunting, so arousing. I slip and slide across skin slick with salty copper. I bed into the folds. Warm. Twitching. I taste the sweetness on my tongue and something moves within me that I haven't felt since before the darkness. Or perhaps not even then...

This quivering flesh pulls me like none other. I think I may be... no, it can't be so. How could I? I don't even know its name. What is your name, my love? My. Love. That feels so right. My love! Yes! I press myself deeper into the damp, throbbing flesh; our screams of delight merge into a shrill hollow that vibrates against the cold, stone walls of our den.

Deeper. It begs me to take it deeper into my cavern. The air thickens with moisture and rot. All sound is muffled here. Its heaving chest is barely a whisper now, barely a soft moan. I like this more. The heaviness. Our forms melt together until I know not where mine ends and my love's begins. We writhe in the euphoria of our shared agony. Oh, what ecstasy this madness brings!

A scuttle? A scratch? A sniff? No! Foul demon! With twitchy nose and whiskers sharp as needles. Rancid fur that hangs on skin-draped bones. Betrayer! Charlatan! Fucking rat!

My lover kicks at it, squirms. It won't have us, will it? I burrow deeper into my love, my soul, and search its heart. The thing is rapid – its spurts tickle my ear, its swells caress my cheek, and I kiss it raw. It moans, ecstatic and in love. With me, only me. It is a lesson the whore rat must learn. It cannot provoke my love to abandon me! The bastard will taste the sweet bite of our fury!

Years it has been, maybe more, since I came to this place. I scarce remember any other. All of my thoughts are of the dark. For a time, I had a pet, a friend. And like most, it was a rat. A filthy, treacherous bastard of a rat. With whiskers sharp and with teeth it poked and gnawed until, absconded, my leg did leave me too. Just like the rat. Just like the light.

And then new friends came. A horde. My horse. My beasties. With legs of twine and silken thread they did give me wings to dance as a moth through my fetid hell. Brought me to the voices they did. Delivered me to my love. Fed me to this stink. Sneaky legged serpents of deceit and fuckery. Luring me into the moist warmth of folded skin and constricting flesh. They brought it to me. They bound its limbs. They whispered for me to taste. Oh... and did I taste! Lost in a sea of rapture so divine I didn't hear the voices. Not at first. First there were just screams. Horrible screams. Then muffled cries and moans. These brought a new sensation, a heat, a pulsing rush that exploded over my skin and twisted my feeble eyes.

I thought our love would last. How foolish. Even in the dark, the blackness takes over. Even my love... my demon. It torments me. Wretched thing. Awful, repugnant, curse from hell! If I had the means I would set fire to the beast and watch it squirm in the scorching flames of my disgust.

And oh! Oh, how they ought to fear my wrath. Let them simmer in the horror of my presence; my shadow stretches far and wide. I've become one with this place, and all those in it are me and mine.

Woe those who enter here, who enter me, for I am a God ruled through the Old Testament. My fury rides on my beasties with a corpsed lover onto me!

ISLANDS OF TREES
by Aiden Merchant

If there was one good thing that came from the Spread, it was that Kirk no longer felt the need to justify his excursions. Life had become one indefinite road trip within the New World, meaning he and Lydra answered to no one but themselves.

Lydra was a German Shepherd. She was four and still youthful, loving, and fiercely protective. Kirk had adopted her from an unwanted litter born down the street from his parent's house. As soon as she was trained, they started taking weekend rides on a regular basis. They loved camping in the mountains, escaping society's rule. Now that the Spread had blanketed the country in large, colorful plants and trees, there was little evidence of the man-made world that once existed, only a year earlier.

Only fourteen months had passed since the initial Change. In the time that had followed, the human population had decreased nearly seventy per cent. With the exotic, unknown plant life came new diseases and animals. Most new things were toxic to humans, which we learned the hard way. People were quickly forced to fend for themselves, but little was edible anymore. Riots broke out. Martial Law was declared. The government fell and our world slipped into a complete free-for-all. People died from sickness and starvation. Others were killed by the new creatures that roamed their backyards. Certain plants released spores into the air that could direct your brain toward violence and hysteria. There were even bugs that were eager to feast on human muscle and bone.

Kirk had learned early in the chaos how to survive. And with Lydra following his every step and command, she'd made it through the Spread as well. Now they were some of the few occupying the New World, which was vibrant in color and dangerous as hell.

Lydra had quickly proven a good guard for the both of them. With many new species to encounter, Kirk could not guess what they would face next. When they first left home, they'd crossed paths with a large, reptilian creature that could camouflage well enough to hide in plain sight from Kirk. It was only when Lydra attacked that he could spot the creature. Its camouflage had gone wild in the struggle, making it visible to Kirk through an array of changing color tones.

They were currently on the road again, or what was left of it. Parts of I-81 had vanished beneath the Change, but Kirk had done well enough finding it time and again over the past week. It was easy to get off track, which had detoured them numerous times already on their trip north. Beginning in Georgia, they were now in Virginia, looking to go as far as Niagara Falls. There, Kirk was interested to see how the Spread had turned things. Global communication was a thing of the past. Even local communication was inconsistent, so it wasn't like he had word of Canada's survival or condition. The last televised reporting Kirk had seen showed the Spread as a global apocalypse for humanity. The next time he looked for an update, there was nothing left to watch. Bombs had dropped across the world, as if they could somehow make a difference against nature's wrath. Kirk was left to assume every nation had crumbled during this blackout. Some days, that seemed overly dramatic. The rest of the time, it seemed entirely possible.

He hadn't minded the Change for the most part.

Aside from losing some friends, the New World had served his interests well. His parents had died in a car crash several years earlier, and Kirk preferred solitude (with Lydra, of course) to human companionship. He didn't like tech all that much, and lived just fine without it. Having to work to pay bills bothered him greatly, and all he really wanted out of life was peace out in the woods, overlooking the shape of the Earth. Now, he had that ability.

As 81 broke apart ahead – trees and large plants sprouting out from the pavement, some standing higher than he could hang back his head to see – Kirk fished out his bottled water and took a swig. Lydra gave him a longing look and he poured some into her mouth. 'Another patch,' he told her, meaning the forest ahead. 'You ready for this?'

Lydra barked.

The patches of growth from the pavement were like islands of trees. Each was unique and mysterious from the outside, deadly on the inside. To go around one would take more time, but sometimes that was simply the safest option. The patch that lay ahead appeared to be enormous, stretching the width of the interstate and then some. Kirk didn't see them getting around it without losing their way in the process.

'Use that sniffer,' he told Lydra. 'Anything foul nearby, get us going the other way. But, just in case...'

He reached over his shoulder and unsheathed a machete. On his hip was also the holster to a revolver, but he left that alone for now.

They began toward the trees.

Had she survived the car crash that claimed her and her husband, Kirk's mother would have loved the flowers of the New World. Ahead, there was one as large as an Escalade, blushing purple, pink, and yellow in a layered pattern. Though beautiful and plush in appearance, Kirk knew better than to go near it. Most of these new plants were poisonous or carnivorous - they'd snatch you like a Venus flytrap and dissolve you in hidden acids.

Lydra growled as they rounded another large tree, this one covered in thick vines that climbed its sky bound base.

Kirk froze and scanned their surroundings. 'What is it, girl? What's coming?'

Lydra lowered her breast to the cracked and dirty pavement (mostly unseen here in the forest) and continued her low growl.

Kirk's grip on his machete tightened as his free hand hovered over the hip holster. He looked at Lydra and tried to follow her gaze. She appeared to be staring down a berry bush about fifteen feet diagonal of them.

'I won't eat any,' he promised, eyeing the dog.

Lydra continued to growl, her eyes intense.

'Is something in there?'

Kirk heard a squeaking from the bush. He waited for more, but there was nothing. Had he imagined it?

Lydra wouldn't budge. Her stance remained poised for attack, her hackles raised and her tail down. Her growl was hardly noticeable now; it sounded more like a forest hum, just a part of the surrounding soundtrack. And then, there it was: the squeaking once more.

Kirk took a step forward. Lydra's gaze broke from the bush long enough to glare sideways at him, but Kirk pretended not to notice.

With his machete held before him, Kirk approached the berry bush. The squeaking increased, almost like a panicked alarm. Whatever was hiding inside sounded young and scared.

Kirk peered into the bush hesitantly and saw something small and furry at its base. He took a knee for a better look, but kept his face a distance just in case. The animal had large, dark eyes and a small, white body. Its fur was puffy, like that of a baby penguin. Kirk didn't recognize it. Either this was the first time he'd experienced the species, or it looked very different as an adult.

'What are you?'

Lydra inched her way to his backside, still grumbling.

The baby animal shook in fear and hugged the base of the bush tightly with little hands. Its mouth was a tiny, pointed beak set just below its large eyes. Its squeaking was that of an immature chirp still in development. At its feet were scattered berries, some of which were partially eaten.

'I think it's a bird of some sort,' he told Lydra, patting her on the head to ease her. 'It appears fairly harmless, but who really knows.'

Lydra looked around them and trembled. Knowing how rarely she reacted this way, Kirk stood and observed the trees reaching above them. Maybe the parents were nearby. He gripped the handle of his machete tightly and narrowed his eyes.

'Is something else out there?'

Lydra sniffed the air and flexed once more, her hair rising on end.

'Shit.'

A horrific screech sounded from somewhere in the canopies.

Kirk retrieved his revolver. 'Get ready, girl. We made something mad.'

The baby in the bushes squeaked louder now, as if calling out.

'Shut up, you little shit!' Kirk hissed, stepping away from the bush.

The screech sounded again, this time from another direction.

'Where is it, girl? Why don't I see anything?'

Lydra seemed just as confused, but still on guard and poised for attack. Then there was the sound of cracking limbs from high up in the trees. Leaves began to fall to the surrounding floor as something hopped from one branch to the next.

Kirk patted Lydra on the backside and told her to run. Together, they fled deeper into the patch, unsure of 81's location. Maybe they were still on it, maybe not. Kirk would worry about that later once they were safe once more. But whatever they had angered seemed to be following them; the groaning of branches continued, only a step behind.

Lydra suddenly took lead and launched herself into

a cavern Kirk would have never seen himself. He followed suit and the two of them huddled along the furthest wall in the shadows, hopefully hidden from the creature above. As they waited for silence, Kirk eyed the surrounding hole and determined it was a pulled-up section of the road. He could see pavement with painted lines in the ruins of the entrance. Outside, the growth had been thick and colorful; it was a good thing Lydra had discovered it for them.

The breaking of branches passed overhead and beyond. Kirk knew better than to stick his head out too soon, and told Lydra to hold position. Several minutes passed without another sound. Finally, Kirk turned to Lydra and asked if she could smell anything. Lydra put her nose in the air and slowly moved away from the wall. When she reached the entrance, she paused and looked around, listening. Then she looked back at Kirk and wagged her tail.

Kirk emerged from the cavern and ran his eyes along the height of the trees. It seemed to him they would later meet this creature if they didn't keep out of sight, out of mind. As he straightened from the climb, he ran a hand down Lydra's back and told her to keep quiet. He then retrieved his compass to get them back on the right path.

This particular patch came to an end not long after leaving the cavern. Apparently, its width had been more substantial than its depth; this worked just fine for them, because soon enough they'd returned to the road and its army of abandoned vehicles. As the duo stepped back into the open sunlight, Kirk raised his head to see if there were any flying creatures above. When he saw the skies were clear, he exhaled in relief. Unless there was someone or something hiding amongst the cars, they appeared to be on a break from danger.

Considering their supplies, Kirk decided they would check vehicles at random for anything of use. In one SUV, the rotting husk of a man remained in the front seat, his skull blown out by what Kirk assumed had been a high caliber bullet. The passenger side doors were both open like screaming mouths, exits for the family but entrances for Kirk.

Inside, he found numerous bags, most of which had been pulled inside out by the shooter. But there were still some road snacks (including chips and crackers) inside, so Kirk gathered what he could and began to eat with Lydra in the heat of the sun.

As his eyes followed 81, it didn't appear that there were any other islands in view. Kirk and Lydra probably had at least a couple miles of pavement before the next patch came along. The day had gotten late into the afternoon and they'd been traveling since sunrise. Soon, they would need to find a place to stop. If not for the corpse in the front seat, Kirk would have set up here at the SUV. But it was far from the only vehicle at their disposal.

They ended up choosing an eighteen-wheeler another mile down. The inside of its cab was large enough for them to both rest comfortably, and it included a twin bunk bed and a microwave. Kirk doubted he'd be able to do anything to power up the convenience, but wasn't really interested in finding out. They had dry snacks and water (and now a case of soda, left in the passenger seat) and bedding to last them the night.

They would be just fine until the morning.

When they climbed out of the eighteen-wheeler some twelve hours later, Kirk was stiff but well rested. As Lydra went to the roadside to urinate, Kirk noted the thick, dark clouds in the sky. It was no wonder they had slept in; the sun wasn't nearly as demanding as it should have been by now. It looked as if a storm was coming, or at least some light rain. Kirk licked his lips as he considered this, none too happily.

There were pros and cons to a storm. They could easily refill their water bottles – pro. However, they would need to take shelter – con. Luckily for them, it seemed that most of the world's new wildlife kept hidden during bad weather. This allowed easier travel, as long as they provided plant life a wide berth; the large flowers had a tendency to seek prey in the rain, their roots becoming animated and dangerous.

As they followed 81, Lydra moved at the head, always ten to twenty feet further than Kirk. A half hour later, the sky had considerably darkened. Further down the interstate, Kirk could see a curtain of rain working its way in their direction. Quickly, he unslung his pack and dug out his and Lydra's raincoats, both of which had been vacuum-sealed to save space. They managed to attach them just in time. The advancing curtain of rain sounded like gunfire now. Within seconds, it was upon them.

'What do you want to do?' Kirk yelled over the downpour. 'Car or keep going?' He looked ahead and still only saw only pavement. It would be a safe journey for a couple hours, at least, albeit a wet one.

Lydra barked and led them forward.

They had gone a half mile when a voice sounded from Kirk's left: 'Don't you want shelter?'

Lydra spun around and returned to Kirk's side, growling at the man she had never smelled. He was sitting in the back of a panel van with the side door slid open part of the way. His clothes were baggy and stained with dirt. His fingernails were long and black, as was his hair.

'It's not her fault,' the man said, seeming to read Kirk's mind. 'I'm wearing the sweat of one of those peace-lily-looking behemoths. Masks your scent real well, I've learned.'

Kirk patted Lydra on the head and she eased slightly.

'That's a new one to me,' he told the man, watching him closely.

'Well, now you know. They sweat in the sun, especially in the afternoon. Rub a little on your wrists, behind your ears... it hides your smell real good.'

Kirk hadn't seen the plant in a long time and asked, 'Are there some nearby?'

The man pointed up the road. 'Keep following the interstate. As if there was anywhere else to go. The next section of growth is maybe a mile from here. That's where I got my most recent batch.' With this, he reached into his coat and revealed a small vial of the sweat.

'Thanks for the tip,' Kirk said, turning to leave.

'Hold up a sec!'

Kirk looked back at the man, his muscles tensing.

'My name is Brodie. What's yours?'

Kirk turned away once more. 'I'm not looking to make new friends, mister,' he called over his shoulder. As he walked - Lydra at his side rather than ahead - he heard the door of the van slide shut. He glanced over his shoulder to see if the man was following them, but he was gone. Likely back inside his shelter.

They continued in the rain, drenched through their coats. Kirk was beginning to shiver from the cold of it, wanting to rest. He found them a car soon enough and they climbed inside for a break. Further up 81, he could see the outline of the next island. If the lily plant presented itself, he would consider bottling some of the sweat himself. Trouble was it could be a trap, and there was no way to know for sure without checking out the plant.

Lydra rested her head in his lap and made her *I'm bored* sound. Kirk chuckled and looked around the car for anything of use. He would love a blanket or some towels, but there didn't appear to be anything useful inside with them. So, he instead looked outside, back the way they'd come. Part of him expected to spot some sign of Brodie, but nothing caught his eye.

And yet, he felt watched.

After an hour of rest, Kirk opened his eyes when he realized the sound of rain had concluded. The skies were still dark and clouded, but the downpour had ceased. Uncomfortably wet, he prayed for the sun to show itself soon so that he could dry his clothing.

They returned to the road and looked around. Still, there was no sign of life within their vicinity. But the patch wasn't far now, so they would have to return to full guard soon enough.

As the patch loomed closer and the sun did its best to fight through the clouds, Kirk couldn't help but consider the man who called himself Brodie. Whatever he'd been wearing to mask his scent was priceless; the question was whether or not he was telling the truth of its source. Under normal circumstances, Kirk wouldn't have given this man a moment, but being caught off guard didn't happen often. Not by people, at least.

With the incredible value of a scent-masking agent,

Kirk would be stupid not to look into the lilies. And if it was a trap? Lydra would protect him and vice versa. Together, they were a strong team that could face off with the risk of a planned attack. Surely, they'd spot the signs – or enough of them to be prepared.

Soon enough, they were upon the island as the sun broke through the spent clouds, warming their backs. They weren't nearly dry, but they were better than before. Kirk wondered if they should take a break outside of the island before heading in; that way they could possibly soak up more sun. The plants weren't going to sweat much until the afternoon, anyway (according to Brodie), so they had some time on their side.

'Hold up, girl.'

Lydra stopped and looked back at Kirk as he came up alongside her.

'Let's rest a bit. Dry off before going in.'

Lydra chose to lie down in the road as Kirk planted himself on top of the hood of a nearby car. After a few moments of discomfort, he stretched himself out with his back against the windshield. The sun was coming out in shards, but was nearly free. The skies in the distance appeared clearer than those directly above. The storm clouds were gradually moving away to spoil someone else's travel.

As they rested, Kirk removed a book from his pack to enjoy. It was *The Hobbit*, a classic he'd read several times over the years. A half hour passed with ease and the sun began to work double-time. After a while, Kirk lowered his book and peered down at Lydra. She seemed to be sleeping, but he doubted that was the case. Unless given the green light by Kirk, Lydra rarely let down her guard to sleep. They had only been up for several hours, and she knew the drill.

A gunshot echoed from somewhere inside the patch, causing both man and dog to jump to their feet. Kirk unsheathed his machete and eyed the trees ahead, which seemed to tower over them like skyscrapers. Lydra scanned the patch as well, her feet firmly planted and her tail lowered.

They watched and waited.

Several minutes passed without a sound. Kirk was about to tell Lydra to relax when another gunshot sounded, this time closer. Then another. Then there was screaming, the kind that came from a man being torn to shreds. It wasn't far, so Kirk directed them back a hundred yards. There, they remained on alert, their eyes on the patch, waiting for someone or something to reveal itself.

Time passed without incident. Kirk relaxed, but wondered what they'd heard. Surely, they'd find out on their way through the patch. He was now hesitant to cross it this afternoon, though. Should they wait around another day to make sure nothing else sounded from the growth? He worried about Brodie and whether he could be trusted. He wasn't too keen on hanging out long enough for the loner to snap and kill them as they slept.

'What do you think, girl?' he asked Lydra.

She looked up at him, tail down, but not between her legs. She seemed impassive.

Kirk looked back the way they came, but saw no one. He then returned his eyes to the patch before them, trying to decide from which general direction the screaming had originated. Was it central to their location, or had it sounded a little more to the west? He considered taking Lydra to the east side for their pass, in hopes to avoid whatever killing had taken place. Then again, he wasn't sure of the location of lilies, assuming they were inside. What if Kirk and Lydra went around the outside border and never found the plant? Then they'd have to double back in search of them, right? Or venture deeper within.

'Maybe we should just kill Brodie for his batch,' Kirk

joked.

'I don't think you'd get the drop on me.'

Kirk and Lydra swung around to see Brodie standing some six feet from them, hands clasped before his groin. He looked smug, or perhaps amused.

'We've got to put a bell on you,' Kirk grumbled.

Lydra growled nice and low.

'That would defeat the purpose of the lily sweat, would it not?' The intruder scratched the scruff of his neck and then clapped his hands together loudly. 'So... did you hear all that commotion about ten minutes ago?'

Kirk simply nodded, watching the man closely.

'Were you hoping it was me in there?'

'The thought crossed my mind, not that I was necessarily wishing it.'

'You're not really the trusting type, are you?'

'Should I be?'

'Why not?'

'Trust, especially blind, is apt to get you killed.'

Brodie chuckled and looked off toward the mountains. He was silent for a long moment before speaking again. 'So, you want to check it out with me?'

'You mean the screams?'

'Yuh-huh.'

Kirk placed a soothing hand atop Lydra's head and gently scratched. Lydra sat and silenced. 'Why would you want to?' he asked the stranger.

'Supplies,' Brodie replied, as if it were obvious. 'Those poor souls probably left behind something good.'

Kirk had him there. Scavenging was a way of survival in the New World, something you were likely to attempt on a daily basis for food and supplies.

'Why do you want to go with *us*?' he asked Brodie.

'Safety in numbers. Even with this sweat, I'm still just one man against... well, whatever the fuck is in there waiting to kill me.'

'The masking isn't good enough to creep through?'

'I'm still visible, am I not? Besides, I do make noise when I walk over leaves and sticks. Not like out here, where I just have to avoid broken glass to get along quietly.'

Kirk had never taken on someone before. It was his and Lydra's way to go it as a duo and nothing more. Still, Brodie could serve as a distraction if they were to find trouble. He hated to think that way – Kirk liked to believe the dangerous New World hadn't changed his moral compass – but he considered it, nevertheless. And if they reached the other side of the patch without issue? Then what? Would Brodie continue on with them as a companion?

Kirk asked.

'We can always part ways when that time comes,' Brodie said. 'I just want to search those remains before getting back on the road. I'm not on any particular path anywhere, like you seem to be, but I keep moving nevertheless. A little that direction, a little this direction. I've been in this general area for a few days now. It's about time to go elsewhere.'

Kirk finally agreed to take the man with them, though he wasn't happy about it. The whole thing seemed suspicious, like the screams had been planned by a friend, maybe someone waiting to trap them. As such, he armed himself and told Lydra to remain on alert. Brodie watched this with interest, but said nothing.

'Well, let's get moving,' Kirk said, directing them toward the island with his machete in hand. Though he could not smell Brodie, he kept his ears out for him as he brought along the rear.

*

For the first quarter mile into the patch, the trio found

no sign of anyone else having passed through. Lydra led them, keeping some ten feet ahead as their guide. Kirk did his best to keep Brodie at his side, rather than behind him; he wanted to have an eye on the stranger at all times and never lose track of him. Brodie had revealed a sawed-off shotgun when entering the trees, and Kirk didn't trust the man not to suddenly turn it on him if he let down his guard.

'Cool, isn't it?' Brodie asked, grinning widely and showing off a gold tooth in the process.

'What is?' Kirk asked, trying not to lose his focus. Lydra was still moving steadily ahead of them, showing no sign of alert. As they walked, Kirk occasionally studied the ground for footprints or spent ammunition.

Brodie displayed his shotgun and stopped briefly to make an action pose.

'Oh,' Kirk said, thinking, *a shotgun won't do you much good out here*. A sawed-off was slow and inaccurate, not to mention limited in ammunition.

'You don't like it?' Brodie asked, matching his walking speed.

'I'm sure it's fun to shoot, but I don't think it's particularly effective out here.'

Brodie looked unhappily away. 'Have you seen

anything yet?' he asked a moment later.

Kirk shook his head.

'Have you heard anything?'

'Just you.'

Brodie stopped and looked around them. Kirk paused as well to watch him closely. Brodie's eyes scanned at level height first, but then his head moved along the height of the trees.

'What is it?' Kirk asked, his grip on the machete tightening.

'I feel like we've gone too far...'

'Why?'

'I could have sworn the lilies were sooner than this. We've been walking too long.'

'Maybe we're off course.'

Brodie nodded and cursed under his breath. Then he squeezed his eyes shut and tried to think. 'Did we enter opposite a '94 Toyota?'

'Not that I recall.'

'Do you remember any of the vehicles beside us?'

Kirk considered that and said, 'We had been resting against a Ford sedan, I think.'

Brodie squeezed his eyes shut again and paced around. Lydra had stopped ahead of them and was looking back curiously.

'Shit. Shit! I don't know where we are.'

'Is there any way to seek out the lilies? Like, by smell? Nearby plant or animal life?'

Brodie licked his lips and said, 'They don't smell. Not that I noticed, at least. That's why their sweat works the way it does. The fucking things use masking agents on themselves.'

'What was around them?' Kirk asked. 'Do you remember anything notable?'

Brodie laughed and clapped his hands together. 'By fuck, I do! About twenty feet over the patch was a black minivan with its side tagged.'

Kirk was no virgin to seeing vehicles pierced in the trees. These new plants grew quickly and powerfully, sometimes impaling things (like cars) and taking them up to the skies with them. If one were hanging by a thread, they could be incredibly dangerous. Kirk knew this from experience.

'That's a start,' he said, looking above them. 'Though, maybe not helpful until we've already come across the lilies.'

Brodie growled. 'What the fuck do you want from me?'

Kirk held his tongue and thought, *I never wanted you here to begin with.*

'If only Lydra could sniff them out,' he sighed.

Brodie laughed suddenly.

'What's so funny?'

Brodie turned to him and removed his backpack. He searched through it for a moment, and then brought out a bandanna. He sniffed it, shrugged, and then held it out to Kirk. 'I got this from the site. I've yet to wear it, and I don't think I've ever sprayed it. Maybe she could get a scent off it?'

Kirk took the bandanna and called Lydra over. 'Only one way to find out,' he said.

It seemed that Lydra was able to get something off the material, because she changed their course and kept her nose low. Keeping up with her meant Kirk couldn't always have Brodie in his peripheral, which was a concern. He hoped they found the lilies sooner than later; he had grown a bit comfortable with the stranger, and he didn't like that. It felt wrong and stupid of him.

They finally came to a clearing littered in human remains. Lydra immediately halted, lowered her head, and began to growl. Kirk stopped beside her and took a look around. The lily patch was ahead – large and brightly colored – but in between them was a massacre. There were unidentifiable shreds of human and animal, bones, limbs, and splashes of blood. Something had to be nesting and feasting here.

'Shit.'

Brodie came up beside them. 'What is it?'

'Take a look,' Kirk said. 'Was this not here the last time you came?'

Brodie shook his head. 'Definitely not.'

Kirk wasn't sure he believed him. 'Well, this doesn't look like the sort of place we should be visiting.'

'Then let's just get the lilies and go.'

'Can we sever them without it compromising the sweat?'

Brodie shrugged. 'I'm not a fuckin' expert on the subject, friend.'

Kirk considered their options. 'Why don't you go and retrieve some sweat while we stand guard.' It was less of a question and more of a command.

'How can I trust you?' Brodie asked, his eyes narrowing.

'I've been thinking the same of you since we met.'

Brodie sighed, grumbled, and crossed to the plant without any concern of the mess he was walking through. Kirk kept Lydra at his side as they scanned their surroundings and listened carefully. As Brodie reached the lily patch and took a knee, a familiar squeaking rose from a neighboring berry bush. When Kirk realized why he recognized the sound, he cursed and retrieved his revolver.

Brodie looked over his shoulder at them and asked, 'What's going on?'

'Be quick and get that sweat. We need to leave.'

Brodie got to work, but continued talking. 'Why? What is that sound?'

'Ignore it and hurry.'

Brodie filled a specimen cup from his pack, and then poked his head into the cluster of berry bushes growing beside the lilies.

'Don't!' Kirk growled, his eyes scanning the trees above them. He spotted the black minivan clinging to the branches, but not the bird creature. Not yet, at least.

Brodie found a squeaking baby a moment later, just as Kirk had feared. 'What is this thing? A penguin?'

'All I know is that it comes with a large parent that hops from tree to tree,' Kirk said, keeping his eyes upward. 'Now, hurry up or we're leaving you behind.'

The furry, white bird began to squeak louder and faster. Brodie allowed the creature to hide once more, and returned to collecting the plant sweat. When the baby continued to screech, Brodie cursed and said, 'How do I make it shut up?'

Lydra began to growl, lowering her belly to the ground. Above them, trees in the distance were now shaking as something approached. Kirk ushered Lydra into the brush and crouched down with her. He hissed for Brodie to hide, but the man didn't listen. Instead, Brodie dug back into the berry bushes to get the baby creature.

'What are you doing, you moron? Hide!'

Brodie ignored him and grabbed the furry animal. Kirk saw what the man meant to do and knew it was time to leave. Brodie was going to get them all killed. But it was too late to run without attracting attention – the mother was above them now, and Brodie had just stupidly snapped the baby's neck to silence its cries. Pleased with himself, Brodie smirked and tossed the corpse through the air like he was making a jump shot.

The minivan shook violently overhead as the mother bird showed itself. Kirk placed a hand on Lydra's back, signaling for her to remain hidden in the brush with him. The creature was enormous and almost pterodactyl-like in appearance. It had feathery wings, but seemed to hop from tree to tree. If it was flightless, that could explain why the last mother they encountered had never followed them onto the interstate.

Brodie had dipped back and frozen amongst the lilies, hoping to disappear. Kirk wondered if the creature could smell him or not. Just because the sweat worked against humans and dogs didn't mean this thing couldn't find him. They knew nothing of these new animals or the power of their senses.

After a brief look around, the mother launched itself onto the minivan and hung its head down to view the bloody clearing. Its neck was long, like a vulture's, and its eyes were sharp and red. The bird was about the same size as the vehicle, which began to dip as the branches beneath it cracked and screamed from the increased weight.

'Be ready for anything,' Kirk whispered to Lydra.

The mother's eyes fell upon the lily patch and widened. Its beak opened wide as it emitted an alarming squeal that pierced Kirk's ears painfully. Brodie shrunk himself deeper into the patch, as if it would save him. It was no use, though, for the mother clearly knew he was there. It began to spring itself up and down on the minivan until the branches cracked and the vehicle began to slide. As it turned to fall, the mother hopped to another tree. The minivan was right above the lilies and Brodie knew it. He tried to run, but rolled his ankle on a severed arm in the process. The minivan dropped onto the patch with the crashing of metal and glass, pinning Brodie to the ground by smashing his legs.

Brodie screamed horribly and tried to retrieve the gun he'd lost in his fall. The mother dropped down from the trees and landed atop the minivan, further pinning Brodie in place. He cried and begged for help, but Kirk knew better than to reveal himself for this stranger.

The mother lowered its head swiftly and bit down into Brodie's arm as he tried to twist and fire his gun. The shot went awry as the mother snapped its beak through, clipping away the limb. Brodie screamed as his blood darkened the surrounding dirt. Kirk turned away, not wanting to see the man meet his gruesome end. He and Lydra needed to leave, but unnoticed. He looked back the way they'd come, but he couldn't forget the lily sweat after all this... could he?

Brodie's screams gargled as the mother tore into his face, removing his skin and nose. It dug into the side of his skull, breaking through his temple and burrowing into his brain. What made it worse was the poor bastard was still alive as the creature took him apart, piece by piece, as punishment.

Kirk scratched Lydra's head to get her attention, and motioned for her to follow him away. They moved slowly and carefully, knowing any sound they made could mark the end for them. He chanced a look back at the clearing just as the mother pecked away at Brodie's open neck. He was dead now, at least.

It was slow progress, but they eventually put some distance between them and the lily patch. Kirk wanted to go back, but not until the mother left. He wondered if that would even happen, but they could check back in an hour or two. Until then, they'd scavenge the rest of the growth; there was no evidence that the massacre in that clearing had belonged to the screaming they'd heard from the road. There could be another body or two elsewhere with supplies.

They began to look.

Lydra eventually caught a scent that excited her, and hurried ahead. Kirk gave chase, all the while scanning the wild and dangerously beautiful foliage for life. Lydra led them to a man-made fort, hopefully long forgotten and abandoned. Inside was an opened bag, which Lydra dug into and found food. As she fed, Kirk looked around them and listened carefully. The fact that a bag was left behind suggested someone intended on returning, unless they'd been killed. He found himself hoping it was the latter.

Once Lydra had moved away from the pack, Kirk checked it himself to see if anything of use was inside. He collected a flashlight and some batteries, but there wasn't anything else that looked important. It seemed likely that the owner had their other supplies on them, wherever they'd gone.

'We should keep moving,' he told Lydra. 'Maybe circle back to the lilies soon.'

Not far from the fort, Lydra found human tracks for them to follow. When she sniffed around the footprints, she looked back at Kirk to let him know there was no scent to match them.

The lily sweat, he thought. Were these old tracks from Brodie, or was someone else using the masking agent as well?

Kirk cursed and scanned their surroundings. 'We'll just have to use our eyes,' he told Lydra as they followed the tracks. There was some uneasiness there, but Kirk also knew they needed to pursue some kind of purposefulness here in the patch; otherwise, why had they come? Just to watch a man get torn to shreds? Something needed to be accomplished. Something needed to be seen through to the end with success.

At one point, they passed splashes of blood across the leaves, but nothing else. Kirk took this to mean that whoever's tracks they were following had been injured along the way. Maybe they were on the run, being chased. Or, at the least, followed. Then again, they only had one set of tracks before them.

Kirk thought of the mother bird. Maybe this person had been her prey earlier. Perhaps these tracks belonged to the man they'd heard scream and fire a gun. Sometime soon, he expected to find a body then (or pieces of one).

When Lydra began to creep, head locked with her shoulder blades, ears down, Kirk took immediate notice. She was coming upon something that made her uneasy. She was showing alarm, but not quite defense. Not yet, at least. Kirk could guess what was coming, what they'd find ahead.

Kirk patted her on the backside, and told her to stay put while he checked things out. Through the brush, he found a rusted and busted sedan with a gory display set upon its hood; a gutted torso sat dead center, and a decapitated head was impaled on a bent windshield wiper. It was the most graphic warning he'd ever seen, aside from the graveyard of limbs he would find from time to time. Those had been left by animals, but not this - this display was done by man.

'Fucking hell...'

Lydra came up beside him, fearful and on guard. Kirk didn't notice her at first, and was a little startled when he realized she was there. Then he laughed, ran a hand through his hair, and shook his head. 'Jesus, who did all this?' He looked down at Lydra and ground his teeth. 'I hate to say it, girl, but... I don't think Brodie was capable of this. There might be someone else out here with us.'

With the internal map he drew in his head, Kirk did his best to make note of the sedan's location. He didn't want to near it again, not only because of the disgusting display, but because the warning could be set outside a base of operations – whoever these people were, he wanted to steer clear of them for as long as possible.

Enough time had passed that they doubled back around to the lily patch, approaching slowly once they neared the clearing. In the surrounding brush, they waited for several minutes in silence, listening and looking for any sign of the bird creature. Once satisfied they were alone, Kirk ventured into the clearing and took a look around.

Brodie was mostly gone, probably devoured. There were shreds and giblets of him, but nothing recognizable. The first thing Kirk did was gather Brodie's things, including the new vials of sweat. With an extra gun now in his pack, Kirk felt a little more prepared if they ran into trouble (even if a sawed-off could only be so helpful). He then turned on the lily patch and did his best to collect more sweat into an empty liter-deep bottle he had in his pack. It was difficult and slow work, and the plants weren't nearly as damp as they had been earlier.

When he felt he'd secured enough sweat (for the time being), Kirk gathered their things as tightly packed as possible, and told Lydra it was time to get back to the road. The day was getting late, and the trees that towered them made it even darker in the growth. Kirk's eyes were already beginning to strain, and that just wouldn't do – especially if there were killers out here amongst the brush.

'I've got an idea,' he told Lydra, searching their things for the little spray bottle they'd found two weeks earlier. He'd considered ditching it more than once, but now it could serve a purpose. He transferred some lily sweat to the bottle, and then sprayed both him and Lydra from head to toe. Normally, he'd use less, but he knew they were already in danger and needed to get moving. The more they were masked, the better.

'Alright, girl,' he sighed, standing. 'Let's get out of here.'

It was quickly getting darker now and they had yet to find a way out of the growth. Two hours had passed and the sun was about to set. From within the trees, it was already difficult enough to see that Kirk had resorted to using a flashlight. He feared they would need to camp for the night, but that was risky under the best circumstances in these wild islands.

Time was growing incredibly short for them.

Kirk was about to give up hope on escaping the trees before nightfall when he finally caught sight of the sunset through the trees. He turned them in the proper direction and hurried Lydra along. He didn't know if the road would be on the other side, but he didn't care. What he glimpsed was freedom, which was enough for now.

Unfortunately, Kirk was moving too quickly and carelessly. A few steps forward and he was suddenly torn off his feet and held upside down five feet in the air, trapped. Lydra began barking at him, upset and unsure of what to do. As Kirk took in the rope around his ankle, he lined up his machete – as best he could, considering the sway of his body in the air – and smacked the rope with its blade. The line was too thick, though, and did not break so easily. Kirk cursed and tried again.

Voices reached his ears. Quickly, he ushered Lydra away to hide. She dove into the bushes back the way they'd come, just in time to evade a trio of men wearing camouflage. One was quite tall and lean. The other two were pudgy with beards; they appeared to be brothers. When the trio neared Kirk, he attempted to strike them with his machete. One of the brothers almost got hit, but managed to step aside at the last second and laugh.

Kirk needed his gun, but his holster was without a strap to keep it in place; as such, the pistol had fallen to the dirt below, out of reach. The shotgun, however, was strapped to the pack on his back. He just needed to swing it over his shoulder without the hunters reacting first.

'You look mighty prepared,' the other brother leered, bouncing on the heels of his feet with a stupid grin spread across his face. 'But not enough to best us. You've been snared!' He laughed loudly and hefted the baseball bat he held at his side. Taking a quick step forward, he took a swing at Kirk, catching him in the kidney. Kirk howled in pain and waved his machete again, trying to reach the man. But the brother darted back as soon as his bat made impact, keeping him out of the way of the blade. Again, he laughed.

'He's got too much fight in him,' the tall hunter said. 'Maybe we should just kill him right here and now. Get it over with.'

Kirk had an idea, but it was make-or-break for his situation. He waited a breath to see what the trio decided.

When the brother with the club stepped closer again – ready for more batting practice – Kirk quickly arched the machete over his shoulder and let it fly. The blade launched at an upward angle into the man's face, carving him from chin to forehead and becoming stuck. As he stumbled backwards – struck dumb by the machete connecting with his frontal lobe – the other two hunters cursed and drew the rifles they carried

252

over their shoulders. But Kirk was faster, having planned ahead. Brodie's shotgun was already in his hands and leveled at the two. Before they could take aim with their own weapons, Kirk blew the head off the tall hunter, blinding his friend with blood and gore in the process. The remaining brother fired his gun in the same instant, but the shot went awry in the explosion beside him. As he danced to the side several feet, startled and shocked, Kirk whistled sharply. Lydra immediately launched herself out of the foliage and onto the chubby man, knocking him to the ground and tearing open his neck with precision. The poor bastard only had a second to scream before he forever lost the ability.

Still dangling upside down and feeling overly strained from his blushing, Kirk cursed his advanced predicament. Now that his machete was elsewhere and his shotgun empty, how was he supposed to get down?

For several minutes, he swung himself from side to side, hoping to reach a nearby tree. When that failed, he tried climbing up his tethered leg and untying the knot. It was no use, though; the knot was too tight around his ankle and cutting into his skin. Carefully, Kirk removed his backpack to search it for something else of use. Somewhere, he had a small knife, used primarily in food preparation. Though he dropped his pack in the shuffling, he managed to hang onto the knife at the last second.

Below, Lydra watched with concern in her eyes and blood on her lips.

Kirk climbed back up his leg and paused for a moment as the red in his face slowly faded. His eyes and head hurt like hell, but he needed to push through if he was to survive this. However tempting it was to close his eyes, certain death awaited. Holding himself awkwardly in place, he told Lydra to wake him if he stopped moving. How much of this the dog understood, he was not sure, but he trusted she'd bark nevertheless.

Finally, Kirk ended his pause, thinking his head would not get much clearer with all things considered. He carefully flicked open his small knife and began carving into the rope. It took a good while, but eventually the threads gave way to his obsessive sawing, sending him to the hard ground below. Kirk groaned atop his back for several minutes, injured and feeling sick. Lydra then stood herself on his chest and licked his face until he summoned the strength to push her away.

'Thanks, girl. I don't think I wouldn't have survived those assholes without your help.'

He stood slowly and patted himself off. Once he'd collected his pack and slung it over his shoulders with the shotgun strapped to its side (freshly reloaded with the remaining two shells Kirk had found in the midst of Brodie's things), he retrieved his machete. The hunter was still alive when he yanked free the blade, but he wouldn't last for much longer. Kirk took his eyes off the man and collected one of the fallen rifles. With it loaded and the men searched thoroughly for anything else of use, he turned toward the light of the sunset they'd followed to this place.

It felt like they'd reached a journey's end. Together, Kirk and Lydra exited the island of trees and returned to the road for their next stretch of asphalt haven.

GRAND DADDY SAGUARO

by Patrick Whitehurst

A shooting star blasted across the southern Arizona skyline. The burning red streak smoldered and vanished in the blackness and left Van wondering if it represented a good omen. He squeezed the steering wheel, keeping the car steady on the ruddy dirt road.

They could not be far behind him.

Enough people got an eyeful of his white GMC Sierra Classic when he drove along the border at sunset. Not many of those beauties out there these days. The pickup, which he called Old Sneaker, dipped into another rut, and Van felt his fillings loosen. The road got steadily worse. He saw only blackness and bugs darting into the headlight beams in streaks of white, becoming stars of a less stellar variety. The insects zipped past his vehicle as if the truck were a starship traveling at warp speed, many becoming specks of greasy blood on his windshield.

Van chanced a look into the rusty, barely connected rearview mirror. Years ago, he'd inadvertently knocked it with a space heater he had been taking to Maria's and busted half the reflective surface out. The things he did for love.

One side of the mirror clung to life and through that side, cracked as hell and spotted with grime, he saw the distant pinpricks of light. Two of them. Far off, but he knew those beams followed his own. Border Patrol on his ass. Bad enough to be a coyote, but to be arrested for it?

As the truck rattled and shimmied along the dirt road, he mumbled under his breath. 'Must have found Ernesto and the others. Pricks talked.'

Only one vehicle in pursuit so far, but they had radios. Soon, others would join in the chase. 'Copters too, no doubt.

Van reached with a steady hand to the side of the steering wheel and flicked off the headlights. The view before him vanished.

'Stealth mode activated, Captain.' After a moment, his vision adjusted to the moonlight.

They would still see his dust trail, but they would also expect him to stick to the road (such as it was) and attempt to intercept him outside of Nogales. Those

Customs dicks always went for the box attack. Always stuck to the playbook. Van had no such formula. One of the things Maria's pops taught him when he first brought Van on a run.

'You get chased. Happens from time to time. Never let them box you in.' When he spoke, the old Columbian's eyes pierced the haze of his cigar smoke.

Van veered the white pickup to the right, felt a large stone scrape the undercarriage, and the rutted road vanished. He let up on the gas pedal, slowing a bit to give him more time to see obstacles, and managed a weak laugh. He didn't need Maria or her pops any more. Shit, he probably knew the desert of the southwest better than they ever did. Not every inch, but most of the country.

Only, he didn't recognize this patch of land.

As he drove further off-road into a soft patch of soil, Old Sneaker went low on the right side. Van gripped the wheel and yanked hard to correct, cursing, and the GMC pulled out like a champ. A fresh cloud of white dust rose into the night sky in an eruption of weeds and pebbles. He slowed into the downward slope of a hill and checked the night sky. Still no sign of a 'copter. Would they come on him with night vision goggles? Heat trackers? *Trek* shit?

Van assumed they would. Not much he could do about it. The looming shape of a saguaro cactus appeared ahead, and he steered around it. Pale spiky arms, a hue of purplish-blue in the moonlight, seemed to wave. Another appeared on his right as the truck ambled slowly down the hill. He spotted a few more in the distance. He'd entered a small canyon. Large bluffs rose around him. The night grew darker, but for Van, safer as well.

He slowed Old Sneaker to a crawl and steered toward a small cul-de-sac of rocks in the bluffs. The GMC skirted a fat three-armed cactus. The spikes scraped the metal in a high-pitched screech that made his teeth clench. The circular indention in the bluff enveloped him. He drove to the edge, nicely tucking the truck at the end of the opening and killed the engine. When he stopped, a cloud of dust washed over the cab and vanished into the night.

'The hell am I?' he asked.

Through the driver's side window, he spied the saguaro that had scraped the vehicle. The thing was close. Lucky he hadn't knocked it under the front end. Federal crime, that one. Protected cactus and shit.

He waited for the dust to settle and tried to trace his exact location. Nogales had to be to the north.

Maybe a bit to the west too. If he went on foot, he would have a better chance of making a motel on the outskirts. The valley would provide perfect cover for as long as it lasted. Stay here and he'd be harder to track. He sat for a few minutes with the window down and listened to the world outside. Something in the dirt made a sort of slithering sound, but he heard no engines. Saw no flashlights and no headlights.

He pulled a black hoodie over his dishevelled blond hair and over his white tee shirt. People never realized how cold the desert could get at night. He'd been with Maria five years, four in the southwest at the border, three helping her dad bring people over. Under, really. Under the damn wall and under the damn border.

When he opened his door, the GMC groaned. Van climbed out, the hood over his head, and stuck his hand into his dusty jeans pocket. He could feel the five grand near his balls, wrapped snugly in his black cotton face mask.

Ernesto may have narced him out to Border Patrol, or Homeland, or *whoever* the hell was chasing him, but at least the bastard had paid first.

The desert air felt cool and still on Van's face. Maybe Ernesto was pissed that he didn't lead the group through the scrub himself. Van had told him up front; once through the tunnel and on American soil, he was on his own.

The man had followed him to his truck with a group of six raggedy women and kids in tow. Van made sure the man saw the Berretta tucked into his waistband. He was not about to be seen driving with a group of illegals in the bed of his truck.

Van shut the door, wincing when it groaned, and stayed rooted to the spot. His ears turned to radar, listening closely, and heard only that odd slithering noise. He turned to face the valley, and he nearly collided into the arms of a seven-foot saguaro.

'Damn thing!'

Heart racing, he angled out of its way and walked a few feet past the truck. The cactus loomed over him, as did a few others, their arms at different angles, and two very nearly embracing one another. They towered in the gloomy, dark canyon like faceless, purple beasts.

He pulled his cellphone from his back pocket. He'd have no signal out here, especially in this canyon, but when it felt safe enough, he could use the flashlight app. Maybe the navigator whenever a signal did creep into his phone. Shit had to work sometime.

He faced east, away from the opening to the valley, before turning back to his truck. Could have been a trick of the moonlight, but there appeared to be more cacti than he saw driving in. So many, in fact, he wondered how he missed them. No beams of light stabbed into the darkness. No footsteps other than his own. Silence ate the night. His lucky day. Ignoring the irksome saguaro, he set off to the east, away from the law.

'Place shouldn't be hard to find again,' he called back to Old Sneaker. 'Don't worry about me coming back.'

His beat-up Air Jordans connected with a wooden board in the dirt. Van winced slightly and knelt to examine the cause of his near tumble. A sign? Out here in the middle of nowhere?

He tapped the flashlight app and ran the white beam over the wooden board. Scrawled in faded paint, more gray than black, he made out the words 'GRAND DADDEE VALLEE' in all caps. The sign had to have been ancient, back from the days of horse drawn carriages and six-shooting desperados, not to mention a distinct spelling style. *Vallee* and *Daddee*. The wood was cracked and swollen with age, almost as grey as the painted letters. Van kicked the sign from his path. He switched off the app and kept walking.

'Captain's Log. Beamed down to the surface of

Grand Daddy Valley and found no sign of life. Place seems more like a canyon than a valley, but what do I know? Scanners indicate hostiles may still be in the area.'

He wondered if anyone would stumble across Old Sneaker, doubted it, and kept moving. For forty-five minutes, Van traveled in darkness. His thoughts zeroed in on *Trek* and Maria. She hadn't been around for a while – nearly three weeks in fact.

Things had changed when she'd met George. *You're still my boy*, she'd said to him last month. Just last month. And then she'd all but ghosted his ass.

Dusty tears itched at the corners of his eyes as he shuffled around a bend in the valley, a sheer cliff face on his right and to his left a stand of saguaro – all twice his height.

He'd probably done one too many Kirk impressions over the years. Forced her away. George drove a Corvette, too. What did Van have besides Old Sneaker?

He noticed more cacti than he had seen at the entrance. Their arms pointed and curved in varying directions, giving them the appearance of ethereal sentries. How they managed to get so tall in the valley he had no idea. Some of them grew over forty feet. What were they, two hundred years old?

He'd come over from the coast with Maria. For a guy accustomed to the beach and fog-kissed cypress trees, the oddly human-shaped cactus intrigued him. Their arms – *apices,* they were called – helped them sprout abundant fruits and flowers. If he remembered correctly, the protected cactus birthed beautiful white flowers at night. Their spines, each around three inches, kept all comers at bay. Those were some nasty things, those spikes.

'Captain's Log. Search database for saguaro flower. We must learn more about this alien species. *We. Must. Mister.*'

For the briefest moment, Van thought the arm of the saguaro closest to him moved. Not much. Not much at all. Maybe a bat fluttered by at just the right moment, but it sure looked like the arm drooped slightly. He saw one of those flowers on the tip of the apice. A bat *could* have been there getting a fix of nectar.

The arm moved again. He had not imagined it after all. It lowered, tipped forward, and the entire cactus ambled half a foot his way. It sailed through the soft soil like a woeful spirit, arms held zombielike outward.

Van choked out a dry scream, gagging, and stumbled away, nearly tripping over his own feet.

Backed into the cliff. Dust fell from the wall of earth, landing in dark clumps on his covered head and shoulders.

They can move? They can't move. Google never said they could *fucking* move.

The cliff scraped his back. He slid sideways, staying pressed to the rock and dirt. Subtle changes were evident in the other saguaro. They too shifted positions. He counted eight of them, some with no arms, others with two and three spiked appendages, and all bearing on him.

Van ran.

As fast as he could, caring nothing for the rocks and trip hazards at his feet. The chilly desert air washed over him. His cheeks flushed and tingled, his thoughts focused only on escape.

He sprinted past a few, but they were nothing more than a purplish blur. As he rounded the curve, however, he found his way blocked by the saguaro. Another batch of the tree-like monsters loitered at both sides of the valley.

He came to a breathless halt. Dust kicked up at his feet. Saguaro blocked his way forward. Tall and dark, they shimmied and swayed directly in front of him. Thirty feet ahead, more and more congregated. Their limbs waved and pointed silently.

He muttered a string of curses under his breath. His pulse raced, beating a drum beat in his neck. Sweat dribbled over his brow.

Captain's Log, he thought, Captain's Log.

No response.

Body tense and ready, Van surveyed his surroundings. The giant plants blocked him at every angle. Their torpid pace brought him no solace. No matter how sluggish, they had him cornered.

He spun in a circle, noting the congestion over every inch of land. The sheer cliff wall would be hard enough to scrabble up without having to get through *them*.

They shuffled in and out of view. Cactus heads bobbed and twisted, creatures with no faces save a blooming white flower here and there. His mind raced. He thought of running. Then thought better of it.

'Do you speak?' Van asked, then louder: 'CAN YOU SPEAK?'

He heard only the slithering, shuffling sound from earlier. They had had him cornered from the very beginning.

He ran his chalky fingers over the hard steel of the Beretta in his waistband. What good would the gun do him? These were nothing more than plants. The hell would he aim at?

He tried a different tact. 'Habla Español?' and heard only silence. *Stupid.*

Swallowing deep breaths full of dust and cold air, he refocused his mind, letting the dirty oxygen tickle his lungs. *Try to stay calm.* He did the same breathing exercises before every border job. It helped drown out the sobs of the children and the questioning Spanish of their mothers. Focus on the action. On the goal. Never mind the noise. Focus on success. Not that he'd had much of that after leaving Ernesto and the others.

Not moving, he centered his thoughts and allowed himself sneak peaks at the cacti army. If they had come any closer, he couldn't tell.

His chest rising and falling, Van let ten minutes pass. Twenty. Had to have been half an hour. What time was sunrise? Soon, he hoped. He wanted a better look at these creatures. Were they wild offshoots of the natural order? The unholy evolution no one wanted?

He couldn't wait for the sun. He had to get a better look. The cellphone flashlight did the trick just fine. Shining it first at the dust-covered Jordans on his feet, he then aimed the beam at the cluster of saguaros blocking his path. Under the light's gaze, they lit up green and bright. A few tilted the stalks at the tip of their heads, as if the bright-white light were nothing more than a curiosity.

'Scanning... nothing to fear, you guys,' Van whispered.

He took a step closer. The plants stayed rooted to the spot. *As if they're normal*, he thought, *but they're not normal. No, sir.*

They looked like every saguaro he had ever seen since arriving in the southwest. Green and bruised, rotten in parts, cactus ribs showing on some, but these shuffled around, arms outstretched for deadly, stabbing hugs. So far as he could tell, they were observing him. They had no faces, only one long body and those plump arms of every shape and size.

He shone the beam high above their heads. A few weeds poked out of the rocky canyon wall. Some areas resembled a rock gym he'd gone to on the coast. He might be able to climb out if he could get to the right spot.

There. His light picked out an area a few hundred feet away. More weeds visible, larger handholds.

The right spot.

Van took baby steps. When he approached them,

the saguaro moved in a circular manner. The ones behind him glided forward, closing the gap. The ones in front fell back. With every five feet forward they dropped back five. Baby steps.

Soon, he found the weedy patch and edged his way toward it. The saguaro backed up, which let him get within twenty feet. But something had changed about their order. To the west of the cacti circle, he saw they had made an opening. The cacti moved aside, pressing against one another to make room.

He saw it then. A shape larger than any of the others.

Towering thirty feet above the tallest in the group, this saguaro needed a lot of room to move. Van turned on the flashlight app.

With at least thirty-two apices, the legion of arms waved and snaked around its fat body, which stayed just as plump and wide from its base to the crown at the top.

Grand Daddies, they were called. The king of all saguaro.

The others moved quickly from its path. A path that led right to Van.

The skyscraper's domain. *Grand Daddee Vallee.*

The King Plant moved with purpose. Faster than

the others had when they'd corralled their prey. As it came into the inner circle, Van ran the light over its body and grimaced.

Impaled on its body like bugs on flypaper were numerous animals. A coyote at its base, desert birds further up, and even large brown bats. One of them squirmed – likely already dead, only its body had not gotten the memo. Leathery wings flapped in a halfhearted, doomed attempt to gain freedom.

The King dropped fifteen arms toward Van, holding them like a boxer in a fighting stance.

Van plucked the pistol from his jeans and stuffed his phone into his pocket. Screw the doubt. He waited a few moments, in which the Grand Daddy glided ever closer, flipped off the safety, and took aim. He only had ten rounds in the clip, and no idea where to shoot, but he'd damn well chip away at the thing.

Van squeezed the trigger, feeling the pistol kick, and a hot zip jumped into the oncoming beast. The slug knocked it back, slowed its progress, but then the hideous thing lumbered forward again.

He squeezed twice. Two shooting flares disappeared into its body. This time the King stopped. Didn't fall over. Didn't squirt green blood and drop dead. The skyscraper just stopped.

'Got seven more rounds, bastard.' To be safe, he backed up to the unguarded section of the valley.

In the darkness he watched the giant sway in place, like a cobra hypnotised by song. Rock and dirt pressed against his back. To his right, waist high, a boulder jutted from the cliff wall just tall enough for him to climb. He'd begin there. The roots of a long-dead tree hung about four feet above it. He needed breathing room if he wanted to mount an escape uninjured.

Once again, he faced Grand Daddy. Two hundred years protecting this canyon, protecting its brethren, or perhaps its children; it knew a thing or two about survival. He'd never heard of creatures like this. Bigfoot, The Loch Ness Monster, even one he had seen on a conspiracy message board. Some sort of ice freak with tentacles for arms, in *Phoenix* of all places. There had never been chatter of living cacti.

He eyed the boulder. If that thing stayed put, he might be able to move fast enough to climb out of reach.

The thought no sooner crossed his mind than an arm measuring twenty feet crashed against the bluff, raining dusty debris across his cheek. Another dark limb swiped at his face, just missing him by an inch.

Van leapt to the boulder just as a third arm

slammed the valley floor. He scrabbled atop the outcropping and lay on his back over the rounded surface, paying no mind to the pebbles and stones pressing into his spine.

With both hands he took aim and fired into the monster. The retorts echoed through the valley in dual thunderclaps. A red sunburst exploded feet away from Van. The first bullet chewed the tip off one of its apices. A second took a chunk of plant meat off its midsection.

Grand Daddy arched back, angling away from him. Another arm swiped over his stomach, missing him by feet, and the creature backed off.

Taking advantage of the situation, Van tucked the hot Beretta into his jeans. He jumped to the roots and grabbed a solid fistful of the stuff. Something clattered to the rocks below. Van cursed. The pistol had stayed put, but he'd lost his cell phone.

Pulling with every ounce of strength, he climbed hand over hand. Sweat dripped from his forehead. He reached the end of the roots, but found a groove in the cliff wall large enough for him to squat in. He stepped carefully into the gap, testing his weight, and finally ducked in. His head brushed the top. The area smelled like rotted plant debris and powdery chalk. He could see a lighter sky above him. Still dark, but less so.

The multi-limbed King filled his vision. He had managed to get just above its height, but only barely. A giant arm struck the valley wall, shaking the very earth with each powerful slam. Another limb soared into the alcove just as he got off a final round.

The apice hit him square in the ribs and yanked loose, knocking the pistol from Van's hands. The great creature fell back. Chunks of green goo hung from the top of its head. The pistol clattered to the valley floor, and he grimaced in pain. He wanted to scream but remained focused on getting higher.

He found a handhold to his right and scrabbled out of the alcove, praying he wouldn't be struck again. He hung from the jutting stone, felt his hand slipping, then found a purchase with his right foot, and climbed a few feet higher. Another tangle of dried brush allowed him to move higher still. With each foot of progress, the earth shook as Grand Daddy beat at the bluff in a flurry of limbs and dust.

Kirk drifted into his mind. *Focus on going up, Mister. Must. Make. It. Up.*

As the terrain became more vertical and the pain in his side throbbed, his progress slowed. He felt as if he'd been stabbed multiple times, the pain arced deep inside him, shooting fire into his heart and lungs. He felt hot blood seeping into his clothes. Above him the sky grew lighter.

When he reached the peak, warmth kissed his face for the briefest moment. Small cobbles tumbled beneath him, falling to the still dark valley and the monstrosities below. Van crawled out, gasping with every pained movement. Sunshine blinded him, its heat weak and young.

He stood on wobbly feet and walked away from the valley's edge. He began to breathe easier. Swollen drops of blood peppered the dry desert floor with every step.

In the distance, a dust cloud rose. The brown mass spiralled high into the early morning light.

Van raised his hands and yelled, then winced in pain and felt the torn shreds of his hoodie. A batch of porcupine spikes were still stuck in his ribs. He could see a handful of tan spikes under his arm pits. They stabbed through his hoodie and tee shirt.

The dust cloud grew. 'Beam me the hell off this planet.' He laughed. Spittle dribbled from his dry, cracked lips. Border Patrol better damn well have a first aid kit and a soft pillow. He had never wanted to sleep more than he did now.

Van pulled the black fabric from the wounds in his ribs and plucked the first spike from the meat with a sucking sound. A tear fell to the desert.

He yanked out the second and third, then got a good look at the blood soaking his clothes.

There was something wrong. The skin had changed colour around the wound.

It had turned a pale, greenish colour.

He pulled the fabric up, ripping it to his neck. The green spread there as well. It expanded in a widening stain. A numbness settled over his entire body. Thankfully, he felt no pain.

'Got me, fucking bastard.'

Van raised his arms again, noticing the coloration on his arms and fingers, and shouted for help. He hopped and waved at the oncoming vehicle. The dust cloud remained close – not so close that anyone would hear him.

The barbs in his ribs popped out on their own and fell to his feet. The colour's hue deepened. Van guessed that his eyes and face were a sickly green. He saw the world through an emerald filter, and he had grown his own barbs. Tan spikes, none so long as the Grand Daddy's, began to appear on his forearms and tear through his jeans. His sight became a thick gelatinous mass, the column of dust visible through a bowl of Jell-O. Torn shreds of jeans and cotton fell in the dirt as his body changed shape and colour like a bulging water balloon in the Arizona desert.

Minutes later, a white flatbed pickup pulled to a stop at the edge of the Nogales city limits. As the engine died, the cloud kicked up by its tires also ebbed and disappeared.

U.S. Customs and Border Protection Agent Jared Steves climbed from the truck. The agent approached a lone saguaro.

The cactus had two arms, both held up as if it were under arrest.

Steves squatted at the base of the six-foot plant. Torn shreds of clothing, jeans, and black sweats lay around his feet. He picked up an intact black cotton face mask similar to the one he kept in the truck. He turned the face covering over and spotted, inside, a wad of bills bound with a rubber band. Steves stood, tucked the roll of bills into his shirt pocket, and returned to the truck. He spoke into a radio clipped at his collar before starting the engine.

Eager to get back on the rutted dirt road to town, and off duty, Steves made his report. 'Thought I saw someone this way. Nothing here now. Heading back.

Over.'

As the white truck drove west, a coyote pranced through the dust and made his way south in search of shade for the day.

He passed the cactus and paused only long enough to smell, then piss on, Van's discarded clothes.

KRODHA

by J.D. Keown

The tigress bounds through the undergrowth, a pair of cubs astride her, fighting to keep pace. Their movements are wild and frenzied, born of desperation and fear.

Somewhere out of sight, a gunshot rings, shattering the stillness and tranquillity of the surrounding jungle. All at once, the brush comes alive: a boar squeals and darts away in the opposite direction; monkeys screech and howl in alarm. Birds of every size and colour career off into the overcast skyline, their intermingled calls a chaotic cacophony.

I perch high above in the canopy and observe as the mother and her children crash across the uneven forest floor, leaping over tree roots and ducking under low hanging branches. The tigress is not aware of my presence, for her thoughts are directed elsewhere, fixed entirely on her sole objective. There is but one thing occupying her mind: *escape.*

Escape, escape, escape. A repeated mantra, pushing everything else from her consciousness. Another shot, closer now, and its ominous suggestion is echoed by a peal of thunder that cracks across the murky horizon.

I hear their pursuers well before I see them, all commotion and indistinct yells. They appear in my grove not a minute later, hot on her trail. A swift headcount reveals that they number eight, and are mostly indigenous Indians. Five of them ride on horseback and carry large pole-arms. From their equipment and manner of riding, I assume these men to be back-beaters in this little hunt. They move in a rigid, practised motion, swiping at anything nearby, whilst shouting and corralling their quarry forward. Two white men ride in a howdah borne on the back of an elephant, and it is one of this duo that carries the firearm, a Winchester repeater. A third, another Indian man, acts as the elephant's mahout, driving it on with a hook.

The tigress moves with such natural grace and beauty, bounding effortlessly over fallen log and through the thicket. However, her offspring are not quite so agile; they are still young and unwieldy, and slow their mother's breakneck getaway down. Were she to abandon them, she would surely make it through.

One of the cubs trips and stumbles, mewling in distress as it strikes the ground. The other pauses, unsure what to do. Its frightened, erratic eyes dart from mother to hunter as it too whines in terror. The tigress stops abruptly, looking back at the humans and baring her toothy maw. She is clearly caught between an impulse to run and a mother's natural instinct to protect.

Fight or flight.

Sparing not a second, the man armed with the rifle slides down from the elephant's back, bolts forward a few steps, and drops down to one knee. He levels the barrel with the rump of the tigress and presses the gun-scope up to his face. With his other eye pinched shut, he begins to squeeze the trigger, gently. The huntsman inhales deeply, but the breath catches and rattles in his chest before the shot is loosed. He retches and accidentally fires the weapon, the crack of the gun ricocheting across the clearing.

The tigress roars out in pain. Despite the misfire, the bullet has found its mark. A glancing shot to the hindquarters, but one that cuts deep, and will likely leave her crippled. If she's to survive it at all, that is.

With a visible limp, she turns tail and hurtles off into the shrub. A wise move, as to stay would surely be suicide. Live today, to fight again tomorrow.

Two of the native men hop out of their saddles, drawing catch poles and looping the nooses over the tiger cubs' heads. Reaching over his shoulder, the elephant driver produces a pair of small cages from within the howdah. He hands them over to his countrymen, and the two young cats are promptly forced inside. The driver takes the cages back and puts them somewhere behind him, careful to avoid the swiping claws of the little animals.

'God damn it!' the hunter hisses quietly. His voice is marked by a distinctive accent. Dutch, perhaps. And yet his dark, leathery complexion and ruddy forehead would suggest otherwise; they suggest a life lived under the ever-present glare of a baking sun. The cut of his clothing is exotic, extravagant. Quite unlikely to be of European origin. Dutch roots, then. A South African?

A salvo of Afrikaans curse words he lets loose confirms it, as he stamps his feet and kicks at a nearby log, like a child throwing a tantrum. Another series of racking coughs assault the man, and he doubles over with a hand gripped around his throat. Intrigued, I study the South African further.

There is something growing within him, I can sense it. Something gnawing and nibbling away inside. A rot, one which runs deeper than his foul demeanour and proclivity for violence. Cancer of the lung, I would presume. The hunter straightens up and pats himself down, searching for something. He removes a handkerchief from inside his utility vest, and wipes the red-tinted spittle from his lips. Then draws a pack of cigarettes, pops one out, and sticks it behind his ear.

'Maybe you're losing your edge, Evert,' the other white man jeers from behind, clambering down from the howdah on the elephant. He descends with far less grace than the hunter, his bulky frame hindering his dismount. By the time he has reached the floor, he is short of breath and flushed in the cheeks. This second white is clearly an Englishman, and probably a relic from the rule of the British Raj in this country. His bearing and mannerisms certainly suggest a man of military background.

The man's posture is stiff as he pulls out a lighter and sparks up a smoke of his own. He strolls over to the one named Evert and slaps him firmly on the shoulder, a nasty smile plastered across his features. 'A poor show, old sport. A damn poor show.'

The South African hawks up a bloody wad of phlegm and spits into the brush, curling his lip and snarling low, beneath his breath. Sweeping the horizon from left to right and then back again, he searches for his prey. His are not the wild and feverish eyes of a creature consumed by bloodlust. No, they are far more dangerous than that – they are calm and calculating. He carries the look of an apex predator. They are narrowed now, and move slowly and methodically, scouring every nook and cranny of his surroundings.

He chambers another round and cocks the Winchester, but does not raise the muzzle. Instead, he tilts his head to the side and listens, ears pricked to the blustery wind. The tigress is crouched down low in the vegetation, her breathing shallow. Though the hunter cannot see her, she watches him intently. Sheer malice burns like fire in that stare, but she remains silent. Neither makes a sound, and the noiseless moment seems to span an eternity.

Another bout of coughs assail Evert, forcing the man to brace himself against the closest tree. He sucks air through clenched teeth, eyes clamped shut and his face scrunched up in a painful wince.

'You alright?' the Englishman asks, though he does

not sound all that worried.

The hunter waves his hand dismissively. His breathing is strained, and he rasps his response: 'Save your concern. I'm fine, Conrad.'

'You really don't sound it, chap,' Conrad mutters, blowing a wispy plume of smoke. He pushes back the brim of his pith helmet and squints up at the dark clouds swelling above.

With more force this time, Evert retorts, 'I said I'm fine. It's nothing.'

'We should leave. We shouldn't be here.' It is the driver who speaks next, but he is not looking at his present company. He is looking directly at me. He climbs down from atop the elephant, but does not shift his gaze from me for even a second. This piques my curiosity. A perceptive fellow, it would seem.

The haunted look he wears implies he has seen horrors that he'd rather forget.

'What on earth are you babbling about, Dinesh?' shoots Evert, scowling over at him.

'This clearing. It is sacred. We have ventured too far; these groves are protected. I think we should leave at once.'

The Englishman spins on his heel, striking Dinesh across the cheek with the back of his hand. The man recoils and raises his arms defensively. His face the colour of beetroot, Conrad points a meaty finger in his face and says, 'You'd do well to remember your place, Mr. Chawla. I do not employ you to think.'

He turns back around and spreads his arms wide to Evert, smiling again.

'Come on my friend, let's get back. We'll go out on the hunt again in a couple of days. We have her cubs. They'll certainly draw in a pretty penny somewhere, so it's not been entirely fruitless,' Conrad smirks and slaps the South African's back again, then adds, 'even if your hunting prowess is still very dubious.'

Evert shoulders the rifle, removes his hat and wipes the sweat from his brow with a shirtsleeve. He runs the palm of his hand through his shoulder-length hair, slicked back and greasy with too much pomade. Levelling Conrad with a cool glare, he runs his tongue along his gums thoughtfully. Evert casts one final glance back into the dense jungle before sighing. 'Fuck it. She won't make it far. Let her die out there.'

I sit and wait in the treetops until I am certain the men are long gone. The tigress is still below me, but has collapsed onto her side. Her breaths come out in pants, heavy and laboured. She is dying. I can feel the life-force draining out of her with each passing second, but she will not perish today. The local man, the one they called Dinesh, he was right. These groves are in my ward. And too long has man's violation of this land gone unchecked. It is high time he paid his dues.

Before anything else, I will need a vessel. A nearby langur monkey bounces on a branch and hoots in agitation. It is distracted, still scanning the aftermath beneath us. This is good. It will not see its death coming. I snake my semi-corporeal form around the boughs of the tree, and ensnare it before it has time to react. The process of possession is swift, but never painless. The host is conscious in the moments leading up to ejection; fully aware of the presence of another being forcing its way inside. The langur briefly screeches in protest and then falls silent, its spirit cast out to make room for my own.

Adjusting my vision to this new pair of eyes, I plot a route to where the tigress is lain below. I deftly weave my way down the huge tree, the muscle memory of my victim making swift work of the descent. Still finding my feet in this unfamiliar meat-suit, I hobble over to the prone tigress. Suddenly she snarls, straining her neck toward me and snapping her fanged maw. I skip beyond the reach of her strong jaws, and note to take care the second time around.

Hush now, I'm not going to hurt you, I whisper, directly into her mind. Surprise flickers in her eyes, but is quickly replaced by sheer terror. The tigress cannot hope to understand me, but she knows enough to be afraid. She paws at the ground and attempts to lift herself up, but is far too weak and collapses once more. Shushing her, I offer gentle reassurances, things that I hope will appease her fear.

You are dying, but I can save you, I murmur gently. *Let me help. Your young need you. Together, we'll get them back.* I feel her heart jump at the mention of her cubs, and know that she would do anything to rescue them. Eventually she calms down, and her breathing becomes stable once again. Reading this as a sign of assent, I crouch down and cautiously place a paw against her haunches. As I trace my fingertips over the open gunshot injury, her muscles and tendons ripple beneath my touch. I marvel at the raw strength that lies there. Such vigour.

After a short while, the bullet rises to the surface and drops out, clattering to the floor. From my open palm, dark tendrils emerge and worm into the opening. Once inside, they begin knotting and stitching the wound back together. When they are finished, not even a scar remains. I stand back and appraise my handiwork, then consider our next move.

Firstly, she will need a name. I ponder it for a moment or two, before settling upon one that feels fitting. *Krodha.* In the native tongue, it means fury and rage. It means vengeance. The word suits her. Right now, this is all she desires, and I will see that she gets it.

The tigress pushes herself off the floor, gingerly putting weight on her wounded leg. She is shocked to find it as good as new, and casts a wary glower in my direction. I disregard it and look around us. The earth is rent and torn from whence the humans came. If nothing else, this path of destruction that man always leaves in his wake makes him easy to track. I set off along the trail, then turn and beckon at Krodha to follow. The tigress falters for a minute, hanging back and looking uneasy. Her mistrust is understandable, but I know her maternal instinct will consume all other reason, so I turn again and continue on alone. Soon enough, she pads along behind me. She is careful to keep some distance between us, though.

*

Krodha and I come across the scars the men have left long before we find their settlement. The jungle here is completely razed to the ground, mutilated beyond all recognition. Trees are ripped from the earth, or hacked down to nothing more than stumps by their metal beasts and barbaric instruments. Wherever one looks, devastation reigns. All is quiet, but the silence is not peaceful; it is thick with the stagnant air of death. Not a single bird sings in this place anymore. The pregnant grey clouds above us finally burst, the rain lashing down in torrents. I look up and examine the sky, lost in thought. It is monsoon season in this country, but will there be enough water to wash away this human blight? To wipe the slate clean of their interference? I think not.

My kind, we brokered a deal with them long ago, back when man had only just taught himself to walk upright. We granted them ample land, and we agreed to coexist. Neither would encroach upon the territory of the other. If only they had held up their end of the arrangement, if they had kept their word, this would not have to happen. But for man, enough is never enough. He is an insatiable creature, and will not rest until everything belongs to him. Or is damaged beyond repair in the process.

After travelling a little farther, myself and the tigress arrive at the edge of a sharp bluff. Down below us, nestled at the base of a bowl-shaped valley, sits the human encampment. Atop a grassy knoll, towering above a sea of ramshackle huts and hovels, sits a lavish walled mansion. I presume this to be the lodgings of the Englishman and the hunter. The shanty town it presides over is haphazard and thrown together; a temporary dwelling for their subordinates. The basin in which the settlement sits is bordered on all sides by steep hills. I take note of this, as it could be used to our advantage. Numerous construction sites dot the perimeter of the camp, and within those lie different breeds of their steel monsters – bulldozers to crush Mother Nature's limbs, excavators to carve out her earthly flesh. Krodha releases a mournful yowl, but I say nothing. I can offer her no words of consolation.

Surveying the scene with disbelief, a question passes through the tigress' mind. She simply asks: *why?* Truthfully, I tell her that I do not know what they are doing here, why they have desecrated this land. Some kind of plantation, drug production, housing development, it doesn't really matter. All that matters now is that we make them regret this intrusion.

Stay here. Await my signal, I whisper to Krodha. She protests with a whine, but a harsh glare in her direction gags her. I hold her gaze until she yields and looks away. The stubborn tigress paces the ridge impatiently. Alone, I begin to descend the harsh incline towards the encampment. As I draw near, I notice a commotion at the bottom of the winding path to Conrad's mansion. I edge forward, careful to stay under the cover of darkness.

Sneaking as close as I dare to in my current form, I see Evert. He is stood, arms akimbo, locked in heated debate with the Indian labourers. Flanking him on both sides are several more white foreigners. Guards, a private militia of some sort, judging by their armament. They carry hefty batons and similar tools of suppression. On their shoulders, machine guns are carried. Dinesh stands at the head of the workmen, one of the caged cubs held under each of his armpits. Their employer is sprinting down from his estate, huffing to himself in exertion. When he reaches the stand-off, he takes a minute to grab some air, hands braced against his knees.

'What the hell is going on? What's all this ruckus?' Conrad spits breathlessly, his face reddened. Equally in indignation and from the short jog down here, I'd wager. 'What the bloody hell are you doing with those tigers, Mr. Chawla?'

'We're not staying one more second. We should not have entered that part of the jungle. Those groves belong to the *rakshasa*.' Just as they had earlier, Dinesh's eyes trail across his surroundings before settling upon mine. I am briefly concerned that he will betray my position, but he flicks his gaze back to the Englishman. 'I'm returning the young to the forest. The spirits there will protect them. Then we're leaving. All of us.' He glances around, but no one will meet his eye.

Conrad does not reply. Instead, he turns and fixes his eyes upon Evert, a wordless exchange passing between them.

In one swift motion, the South African slips a bullet into his rifle, cocks it, and shoots Dinesh.

The man's chest spurts blood from both the entry and exit wound; a clean shot. One directed at the heart, and aiming to kill. Dinesh drops the cubs to the ground, falls backwards with a surprised grunt, and tumbles head over heel into the roadside ditch. His groans and wails of anguish don't start until he hits the earth with a thump. Conrad clicks his tongue loudly, his beady eyes flicking from face to face. 'Does anyone else wish to raise any objections?'

Were it not for the rainfall, one could likely hear a pin drop in the quiet that follows. The men look from one another, shifting from foot to foot, but no-one dares utter a word. Some of the men move to assist Dinesh, but their employer tuts and waggles his finger slowly. Another uncomfortable silence falls, and stretches out even longer than before. Eventually, the labourers exchange guilty glances and back down.

Conrad nods his head, apparently satisfied that the matter is put to bed, then clicks his fingers and points in the direction of the cages. Evert hands his rifle to the closest guard, then strides over to the imprisoned tiger cubs. He hauls them up from the floor, and then he and Conrad head back up the dirt road towards the mansion. The workmen watch them leave, thinly-veiled resentment written in their expressions. They disperse among the shacks that make up the improvised shanty town.

Now is our time to strike. Keeping to the shadows, I slink down into the trench. Dinesh twists and writhes as I approach him, coughing blood into the soil and moaning softly to himself. As I did with Krodha, I whisper words of comfort into his mind. He needs not know that they are empty and meaningless.

His life could be saved too, but I need him for another purpose now.

Abandoning the langur, I slip into his body with ease. He was close to death regardless, and in the short flash that we occupy his being at the same time, I know that he welcomes its bitter embrace. As they always do, his soul screams in indescribable agony for a few seconds before I expel it permanently into the ether. The empty husk of the monkey crumples into a steaming pile of flesh and bone, sizzling as it seeps into the earth. Adapting to this new vessel, I scurry out of the ditch and scan the area. There are at least a dozen guards, and twice as many workers. If we are to succeed, I will need to tilt the odds in our favour.

Spreading my arms to the sky, I begin to ramble in an ancient tongue, unknown and utterly incomprehensible to man.

The rain pours heavier and heavier, gushing and bubbling down the slopes of the hills in great, muddied waves. The soft, sandy earth gives way beneath the powerful flow, and the slurry slides into the valley with an almighty rumble. Panic spreads like an infection among the humans as they realise what is happening, terror etched into the lines of every face.

They are right to be afraid. A disaster like this was

bound to happen sooner or later, and it is obvious that they are poorly prepared for it. Mother Nature is a fickle, tempestuous mistress. Though man tries to break and bend her to his will, she will always persevere and come out on top. This place embodies his arrogance, and the lack of respect he shows her will be his undoing.

The militiamen have noticed me now too, and cries of alarm begin spreading among them. I cast my head back in the direction of the ridge, and call out as loudly as my dead lungs can muster. A few of Conrad's soldiers reach for their weapons, but Krodha hurtles down the bank and is upon them before they make it halfway. She carves a bloody swath through their number, slashing and mincing through them as though they were made of paper.

Swiftly forgetting their loyalties, the indigenous labourers drop whatever they are doing and begin fleeing down the highway out of the camp. The militiamen are blinded by their own obedience, and try to rally them and restore order. Their actions are in vain, as the frenzied chaos of the wild storm and sudden ambush demands their full attention. I let the workmen go. They may have had a hand in what was going on here, but they are not to blame.

I scurry forward on all fours, catching one of the guards by surprise. The man shrieks at the bizarre sight of the reanimated corpse bounding like a dog. I leap upon him and gnash my teeth an inch from his face. When I connect with his neck and start tearing, the blood pumps out like a geyser. My human teeth pale in comparison to Krodha's fangs, and seeing her claim revenge is a truly beautiful thing to behold. She rends the guards apart, her massive paws cutting their torsos to ribbons, her jaws swinging their lifeless bodies around like mere rag-dolls.

Those that are slaughtered by tooth and claw are the lucky ones. They who attempt to flee suffer a far worse fate. Most are buried alive beneath the landslip, the mud-water filling up their throats and snuffing out their screams. An especially unlucky few are dragged along by the current; they are battered and mashed to a pulp by the turbulent flow. I whistle to Krodha, pointing my finger up the trail to the estate. She takes the lead and together we ascend. All around us, the mudslide crashes through the temporary shelters and construction sites, sweeping everything in its path away.

Perhaps this land can be cleansed after all.

We pass under a grandiose archway and enter a

sprawling courtyard. Krodha catches sight of our quarry before I do, and surges on before I am able to stop her. The two men have not yet made it indoors by the time we catch up to them. They are running from the cloudburst, and are just about to climb the steps of the house's wraparound veranda. Krodha's young start chattering excitedly at the sight of their mother.

The pair turn around in unison, but the expressions they wear are polar opposites. Conrad blanches as his lower lip and corpulent jowls tremble. Evert gently places the caged cubs onto the wooden planks of the veranda, his eyes never straying from us.

'What in God's name –' is all Conrad can manage, before he clutches at his chest with both hands. The look of horror on his face contorts into a grimace of pain, and he collapses in a heap. Unconscious or dead, I do not know. Rolling his eyes, Evert drops down to one knee and feels for the man's pulse. Then mutters a curse under his breath.

Evert casts his hat aside and vaults over the bannister of the wraparound, his boots hitting the wet earth with an audible squelch. He no longer carries his rifle, but draws a nasty-looking kukri knife from a sheath strapped across his chest. Stalking into the courtyard, the hunter holds the blade aloft with both hands. He shakes the rainwater from his vision like a wet dog. *It is high time this mongrel was put out of its misery*, I think, a sentiment which is echoed by Krodha.

I notice that his knuckles are bone white, and his eyes have completely lost their cold, emotionless edge. Wide and fearful, the irises are pinpricks against the whites. They are no longer the eyes of the predator. Now, he is the prey. Evert circles around Krodha, and she mimics his movements. This battle dance continues for a few minutes, though it feels like hours pass. Time slows to a trickle in the confrontation, neither party wishing to strike first and surrender the advantage. The deluge continues, the sky almost black with angry clouds. Beyond the walls of Conrad's estate, the mudslide has become a seething river. It heaves with a flotsam of bodies and debris.

Whilst the two are distracted, I drop this human vessel to the ground and slither like a serpent up to the cages holding Krodha's offspring. The hunter is too preoccupied with the tigress to notice me releasing them. I try to scoop up the infants, but they wriggle free from my awkward grip, the onset of rigor mortis starting in this shell.

They scamper away, eager to assist their mother, and suddenly Evert yells out in shock. He spins around to find one of the cubs with its jaws clamped around his ankle. A well-placed blow from his boot sends it hurtling with a pained yelp, and Krodha roars her distress. Before the hunter can turn back to face her, the other begins to nip at his heels and tear on his trouser-legs. Their tiny fangs are little more than an annoyance to him, but they succeed in drawing his attention away from the mother for long enough.

Evert raises the kukri high above his head, lining it up with the neck of the nearest cub. Before the blade can fall, the cancer growing within him makes itself known again, and he stumbles off-balance. Flailing about, he does not see the tigress as she creeps around his left side. Nor does he see her pounce in for the kill.

Krodha's jaws find his throat, and clamp shut with a satisfying crunch. Evert's body sags in the powerful, vice-like grip of the tigress's maw. She quickly spits him back out, as if the rot in his heart has spread through the meat on his bones. Her robust body trembles as all the rage and frenzy bleeds out of her. She shivers, blinks several times and then glances around. Her expression is vacant and slightly confused, but all the bloodlust has gone from it. As though in sync, the violent downpour begins to ease, before stopping entirely.

*

The cubs prance over to their mother, but their joyous reunion is delayed a fraction longer. Krodha's ears flatten, and she lets out a low, rumbling snarl. Such a clever girl. She has found a lone survivor, someone I had overlooked somehow. Searching the camp, we find him cowering in an outhouse. A flimsy wooden door separates us, but we can hear his pitiful whimpers through it. I tear the door off of its hinges and cast it aside, and the militiaman screams until his vocal cords are hoarse. Krodha's roar is louder still though, and I see that he has voided his bowels.

The tigress lowers herself to a crouch, preparing to lunge. I carelessly wave my hand and, speaking into her head, I order her to stay. She grumbles her annoyance, but does as commanded and paces behind me. The man springs up from the toilet seat, hitches up his trousers and bolts down the road heading southward, back to civilisation. I can feel Krodha's eyes burning into the back of my head; she questions why I would show mercy now.

Let him go. Let him tell others what he has witnessed here. Let those others extend the hearsay and whispers further, and let those rumours take hold and spread like a wildfire. Maybe they'll think twice before coming back. Krodha roars once more, mighty and ferocious, compelling the man to flee faster. He stumbles over his own feet and cries out in panic, before scrambling up and darting down the highway quicker than I've ever seen a man move.

We watch him disappear on the horizon. After he is out of sight, the tigress turns her attention to her cubs, and all her aggression melts away. Reunited at last, Krodha nuzzles them both and purrs contented. I wheel around slowly, satisfied with the panorama of chaos the two of us have wrought. Then I make to leave. Now several metres ahead of me, Krodha guides her young from our carnage. She is heading north, deeper into the jungle, and further away from man and his appetite for destruction. She is smart to do so. I sincerely hope that she will be far from here by the time the humans return.

Krodha stops once she reaches the edge of the clearing, and her cubs look up to her in confusion. Their attention is not held for long, and soon they are play-fighting with one another, tumbling through the undergrowth and yipping in their funny game. The tigress ignores them and stares back at me, a mix of emotions painted in her eyes. There is fire and flame there. A bravery that burns deep within her heart. But she is also afraid. Terribly afraid. I probe inside her mind, and it is in just as much turmoil. Despite all we have been through, she still does not trust me. She fears I will pursue them.

There it is again. Fight or flight.

Her urge to run is palpable, but for the briefest moment she considers attacking me. This thought passes as quickly as it appears, though. She understands that that would be a very foolish idea. A clever girl indeed.

I raise Dinesh's dead and broken arm in a farewell gesture, twist his dried, bloodless lips into an imitation of a smile. Her eyes linger for a beat, then she turns away and growls at her cubs to come along, and they obey without hesitation. The three disappear into the gloomy treeline, and I am alone. The silence rules once again.

Picking my way carefully through the wreckage, my attention is drawn to a furrow carved into the damp mud. I follow the track like a bloodhound on a hunt, and am surprised by what I find. Conrad. I shake my head in disbelief. Another oversight on my part, but this one is a delightful treat. He squirms like a fat, pathetic slug, gasping out for breaths that refuse to come.

I watch the Englishman crawl across the sodden earth, gripping his chest with one hand and clawing himself forward with the other. Craning his neck around, he screams and thrashes wildly upon seeing me approaching. With little exertion, I hoist him from the mire and drag him alongside me by the scruff of his collar. I feel him quiver, hear the sobs escape his lips. He whines quietly for a minute or two then goes slack, resigned to his fate. Oh, if only he knew what I had in store, he may not come so readily.

He'll make an amusing plaything for a while, at least.

I muse on what I'll do once I'm finished toying with the man, relishing the many possibilities. Maybe I'll pluck out his soul and pick it apart atom by atom. Perhaps I'll string his body up by the roadside, a crude testament to our vengeance. A warning, to those that might think to follow in his footsteps. Or I may choose to simply wear his skin, and lie in wait until they arrive. When they do, I'll jump out of the brush in Conrad's rotting corpse, and show off our diorama of death like some demented ringmaster.

And more will come, they always have. They will not stop until all the marrow from Mother Nature's bones is sucked dry. They'll be back to disfigure further, to violate, to vandalise. Greedy locusts, stripping this land bare.

But it's no matter. I'll be right here waiting for them.

ACKNOWLEDGEMENTS

Thank you to everyone who made this possible, and who's supported not only *Wild Violence* but *Blood Rites* so far. The readers, writers, reviewers – let it never be thought that your support has gone unnoticed, because it all means so much to me, especially with these charity anthologies.

Thank you also to my wonderful partner, who has been supportive and helpful through all the stress of putting these books together; and to the circle of writers and friends who have been instrumental in helping me to make it happen.

Thanks to Spencer, as always, for giving everything one final look and catching many of the mistakes I tend to miss. My job is a lot easier for your support.

Don't forget to keep a lookout for more

anthologies and books from *Blood Rites,* and leave a review where you can. They help so much, and it's so, so important to get the word out there about these anthologies so that we can raise as much money as possible for the wonderful charities we're hoping to support.

Thank you.

Nick Harper

AUTHORS

SPENCER HAMILTON

2020 saw the publication of Spencer's first book, the short story collection *Kitchen Sink,* and his debut novel *The Fear,* which Mother Horror called "a sweet-spot for the supernatural and body horror" and The Lesbian Review called "psychologically upsetting and physically ghastly". His newest work, the slasher novella *Welcome to Smileyland,* will be available in the spring of 2021.

You can find him at www.SpencerHamiltonBooks.com or on Instagram (@nerdywordsmith) or Twitter (@SHamiltonBooks), where he is occasionally clever. He lives in Austin, Texas.

MOCHA PENNINGTON

Mocha Pennington studied journalism with a minor in creative writing at college. Her short story, "Cedar Road", was featured in *Secret Stairs* and "Liked" was featured in *The One That Got Away: Women of Horror Anthology Vol. 3*, both of which saw #1 on Amazon in the horror anthology category. She separates her time writing her first novel and co-hosting Tea Time, a gossip channel on YouTube.

Don't be scared to follow her:

Twitter: **@Mocha_Writer**
Instagram **@MochaPenn**
YouTube: **youtube.com/c/teatimexoxo**

L. PINE

Being partial to a perfect blend of horror and humour with a penchant for monsters, L. Pine enjoys delving into the weird and peculiar side of media, inspired by the works of Jan Svankmajer and Jim Henson. She focuses on writing, painting, and drawing as a means of creative escapism to replenish her energy. As a recent graduate of the University of North Texas she is currently grappling in a valiant effort to make a living that will excuse her Bachelors of Fine Arts degree. L. Pine lives mostly alone, kept company only by a hoard of well-loved ghosts from pets past who have refused to move on because their lives with her were way too good.

Her artwork can be found on Instagram under **@ghosthoarder**. Her latest story, "A Pleasant Family Visit", can be found in the Dead Fish Books' *Universe of Attractions* anthology on Amazon.

MICHAEL R. GOODWIN

Michael is the author of *The Liberty Key,* a novel of supernatural suspense, *Smolder,* a horror novella, and *Roadside Forgotten,* a collection of five short stories.

He lives in Maine with his wife and four children. Follow him on Instagram **@michaelrgoodwin** or visit his website, **www.michaelrgoodwin.com.**

CARLA ELIOT

Carla Eliot is a UK writer living in Cheshire with her young son and little dog. She enjoys writing moody fictional stories, often encompassing an underlying message and frequently diving into the paranormal. Carla featured in the previous two Blood Rites anthologies with her stories, "My White Star" and "Windows to Your Soul". Two of her other short stories have been accepted by separate indie presses and these will be published later in 2021. When Carla isn't writing, she's usually reading, enjoying nature, or watching films.

Website: **carlaeliot.com**
Instagram: **@writecarla**
Twitter: **@writecarla**

K.A. SCHULTZ

Author-Illustrator K.A. Schultz "writes with pictures
and draws with words." To learn more
about the author, her articles and literary or
illustrative works, please visit
www.butterflybroth.com and
www.jacobmarleystory.com

@butterflybroth
@jacobmarleystory

GRACE REYNOLDS

Grace Reynolds is a writer of dark poetry and often dreams up macabre scenarios that are inspired by the mundane realities of life. Originally from the great state of New Jersey, she now lives in Texas with her family and is currently working on her debut collection of poetry. When Grace is not writing she is reading or attending to the daily responsibilities of a domestic engineer.

Connect with Grace at **www.spillinggrace.com** or follow her on Instagram **@spillinggrace.**

SARAH ROBERTS

Sarah Roberts is the author of the upcoming psychological thriller Hollow, co-author of the novel *Rokula*, as well as a contributing author and editor of two anthologies: *Seven Deadly Sins - A Horror Romance Anthology* from The Fringe, and *Seven Heavenly Virtues - A Fantasy Noir Anthology* from The Fringe. In addition to writing, she enjoys gardening, painting, sculpting, and taxidermy.

You can explore more of Sarah's work here:
www.authorsarahroberts.wordpress.com
www.therokulasaga.wix.com/rokula

On Instagram :
@anythingispossibleifithappens

MICHAEL BENAVIDEZ

A reader first and writer second, Michael Benavidez spends most of his time reading rather than writing. Taking his platform on Instagram as a place to review books within the indie market (as well as through the monthly column *You've Got Read on You* at Morbidly Beautiful), he is set to help spread the word of the underappreciated work in the ever-growing sea of indie horror.

As a passion and hobby rather than a job, Michael Benavidez takes care in creating stories with meaning and grit, touching on the horrors that the world has presented to him over the years. Currently he has two short stories available: *When Angels Fail* and *As the Shadows Grow.* He can be found on Instagram **@wafmichael** currently, enjoying the low-key fun of limited social media.

AIDEN MERCHANT

Aiden Merchant is an author of horror, suspense, and crime. He grew up on *Goosebumps* and *Scary Stories to Tell in the Dark,* before graduating to Stephen King as a young adult. He now reads a plethora of authors, many of whom flourish in the independent horror community.

Since 2019, Merchant has released three story collections, co-edited a charity anthology (*Black Dogs, Black Tales* – Things in the Well Publishing), and appeared in a Blood Rites Horror anthology (*Wild Violence*). In 2021, he will finally release his ten-episode screenplay series, *Love&Eyes,* which tells the gritty backstory of his popular character, Gina Charter. In 2022, another new horror collection is prepared for publication, as well as a novel or two.

You can follow Merchant on Instagram, Twitter and **www.aidenmerchant.com** for the latest in news, reviews, and releases. Though quiet, he is very friendly and likely to respond.

PATRICK WHITEHURST

Patrick Whitehurst is a fiction and nonfiction writer. His recent nonfiction book, *Haunted Monterey County,* reveals the many ghostly locations found along the California Centra Coast. A fifth nonfiction book, *Murder & Mayhem in Tucson,* will be published in late 2021. His fiction includes The Barker Mysteries novellas as well as short stories in the horror and crime genres. His short fiction has appeared in numerous magazines and anthologies, including *Bitter Chills* from Blood Rites Horror. His book reviews and author interviews can be found at Suspense Magazine. Patrick's books and short stories can be found on Amazon.com.

As a former Arizona journalist, he covered everything from the deaths of nineteen Granite Mountain Hotshots to President Barack Obama's visit to Grand Canyon.. Patrick strives in his writing to normalise the grey areas found in everyday life.

Find him online at **patrickwhitehurst.com.**

J.D. KEOWN

Joshua Keown lives on the outskirts of the North York Moors with his feral little hound of hell, Lola. Despite his proximity to Whitby and a lifetime aversion to being out in the sun, he would like it to be known that he is definitely not a vampire. Josh is an avid enthusiast of the horror genre in all its forms, and has recently turned his attention to writing ghastly, ghoulish stories of his own.

His debut novella *Maggot Brain* is coming soon, and the full details can be found on his personal site at **www.nightterrornovels.wordpress.com**. Josh prowls almost every corner of the internet in some capacity, but is most easily reached on Instagram and Twitter under the handle **@JDKAuthor**.

Printed in Great Britain
by Amazon

61725757R00190